網羅最實用的**核心英文句型**，
搜尋文法、快速抓住重點，就靠這一本！
讓滿分筆記帶給你滿分英文！

User's Guide 使用說明

祕訣 **1** 概念式主題講解核心句型

本書按概念式主題分為 7 個單元,從「動詞時態與分詞變化」、「形容詞與關係詞」、「子句與五大句型」、「常用句型」、「假設語氣」、「倒裝句型」到「It 的相關句型」,每單元內的細項概念難度循序漸進遞增,從簡易到進階將核心句型一網打盡。

祕訣 **2** 大量例句示範文法重點

全書句型重點皆以大量例句示範講解,讓讀者直接從例句觀察文法使用模式,不怕看不懂句型說明,學習更直觀,效果更顯著。例句撰寫用詞簡單實用,貼近日常生活,讓讀者在學習句型文法的同時,可以在生活中運用所學知識。

祕訣 **3** 即時測驗鞏固學習成果

每個句型重點後面皆附「即時測驗」,幫助讀者學完一個部分就可以馬上檢視學習成效。每單元最後還有「綜合練習」,驗收各單元學習成果,找出學習盲點,全方位掌握章節重點。也幫助讀者鞏固記憶,加深印象,將英文句型知識內化活用。

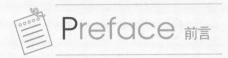

Preface 前言

在這個國際合作愈發緊密的時代，外語能力儼然成為職場的必備技能之一，而英文作為最被廣泛使用的語言之一，自然成了許多人的第一外語首選。不論是外出旅遊、升學求學，還是求職轉職，良好的英文能力都能在各方面帶來絕佳的優勢，相信這也是大多數人學習英文的動機。

那麼，想學好英文，我們可以怎麼做呢？要學好一個語言，除了有足夠的單字量以外，更重要的是能夠理解一個語言的規則，並將其運用自如。因此，想要在試場中奪得高分、在職場上來去悠然，只會死背單字是遠遠不夠的。不懂得用英文的邏輯思考，就很容易說出中式英文，甚至在語意上產生偏差，造成誤解。

本書集結了作者的多年教學經驗，劃分成七個章節講解句型觀念，並在章節學習過程中穿插小測驗，方便讀者更了解自己的學習成效、抓住學習重點。只要抓到關鍵學習重點，並且跟著本書的腳步按部就班走，一定可以輕鬆理解看似複雜難懂的句子，在英文學習上攻無不破！

英文句型不難學，只要我們以開闊的心去看待它，不將其視為洪水猛獸，就會發現英文句型的有趣之處。希望本書的讀者們在閱讀本書的過程可以收穫滿滿，發覺學習英文的樂趣，並建立自信勇敢開口說英文。

Contents 目錄

Chapter 3 子句與五大句型

Chapter 4 常用句型

Chapter 5 假設語氣

Chapter 6 倒裝句型

Chapter 7 It的相關句型

Chapter 1
動詞時態與分詞變化

Part 1 | 現在式

　　英文跟中文最大的差異點之一即在時態。中文敘述中，只要在時間闡明即可，但是英文卻不只要有時間副詞，還需要有動詞變化。動詞的變化中，會受時間基點跟動作形式影響，所以總共會有12種變化。我們會在以下的章節一一說明。

★ 時態區分法

時間 動作形式	現在	過去	未來
簡單式	現在簡單式 **I walk.**	過去簡單式 **I walked.**	未來簡單式 **I shall walk.**
進行式	現在進行式 **I am walking.**	過去進行式 **I was walking.**	未來進行式 **I will be walking.**
完成式	現在完成式 **I have walked.**	過去完成式 **I had walked.**	未來完成式 **I will have walked.**
完成進行式	現在完成進行式 **I have been walking.**	過去完成進行式 **I had been walking.**	未來完成進行式 **I shall have been walking.**

　　準備好了嗎？那我們就趕緊進入第一個說明：現在式！

 現在簡單式及現在進行式

一、現在簡單式的使用時機：

1. 表示永恆事實、不變真理

● Boiling-hot water evaporates quickly as steam.
滾水很快就蒸發成水蒸氣。

- Ice melts completely at a temperature just above 0°C.
  溫度只要超過攝氏零度，冰就會融化。

2. 格言諺語

- There is no place like home.
  沒有任何地方像家一樣。

- God helps those who help themselves.
  天助自助者。

3. 表示習慣或反覆的動作，常與以下頻率副詞連用

❶ always / often / usually / sometimes / seldom / frequently

❷ every＋時間

❸ 次數＋時間

- Sara always uses social networking apps to contact with her friends.
  莎拉總是使用社群網路應用程式和她的朋友聯繫。

- She travels abroad once a year.
  她每年出國旅遊一次。

- My aunt volunteers to clean up the beach every Saturday morning.
  我阿姨每個星期六早上志願去清理海灘。

4. 表示時間或條件的副詞子句，用現在式代替未來式。

（「來去」動詞：come/ go/ fly/ return/ arrive/ leave代替未來）

- If he lies to me, I will break up with him.
  如果他對我說謊，我就和他分手。

- Kevin will host the meeting tomorrow morning.
  = Kevin hosts the meeting tomorrow morning.
  凱文主持明天早上的會議。

二、現在進行式（am/ is/ are＋V-ing）的使用時機：

1. 表示目前或說話時正在進行的動作常與以下副詞連用：

❶ now / right now

❷ at this time / at present

❸ at the moment / for the time being

- **Fiona is solving the math question now.**
  費歐納正在解這道數學題。
- **The child is peeking into the room.**
  小朋友正在往房間裡面偷看。

2. 表示「反覆發生」或「老是……」之意。搭配的副詞列表：

❶ always（總是）

❷ constantly（不斷地）

❸ continually（不停地）

❹ forever（不斷地）

❺ perpetually（不斷地）

❻ repeatedly（再三地）

- **Gary is always making excuses, so no one would trust him anymore.**
  蓋瑞總是在編藉口，所以沒有人會相信他了。
- **Why do you constantly pick on him?**
  你為什麼總是找他麻煩呢？

統整小教室

- **Why are you using a tablet computer?**（→正在發生的事）
  你為什麼現在在用平板電腦？
- **Why do you use a tablet computer?**（→個人習慣）
  你為什麼習慣用平板電腦？
- **I live in Prince Edward Island.**（→表達事實）
  我家住愛德華王子島。→ 可能是指我的老家，不是我現在人所居住的地方。
- **I am living in Prince Edward Island.**（→正在發生的事）
  我現在住在愛德華王子島。→ 我的現居地，可能是在外地工作居住的地方。

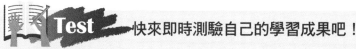

Test ——快來即時測驗自己的學習成果吧！

( ) 1. She never _____ up after her dog.

(A) picks (B) picked (C) pick (D) picking

( ) 2. If her income _____, she will definitely be able to improve her quality of life.

(A) increased (B) will increase (C) increases (D) has increased

( ) 3. For the time being（目前）, the viewers _____ to enter the seating area.

(A) wait   (B)waited   (C) are waiting (D) will wait

( ) 4. An average sized lobster _____ about 2 to 3 pounds.

(A) have weighed (B) weighs (C) weighed (D) are weighing

( ) 5. It is said that wildfires _____ in Australia during the dry season every year.

(A) appeared   (B) appear (C) are appearing   (D) has appeared

解答：(C) (C) (C) (B) (B)

 現在完成式及現在完成進行式

一、現在完成式

　　現在完成式用以表示從之前到現在為止的經驗或做過某個動作的次數，或表過去到現在的動作、性質、狀態，或表過去的努力，今天的成果。是英文獨有的時間觀念，中文沒有。現在完成式的使用時機：

1. 表示動作的完成：常與already/ just/ yet等副詞連用。

● Has Kevin handed in his report yet? 凱文繳交他的報告了嗎？

● I have already bought latest album of BTS.
我已經買了防彈少年團的最新專輯。

2. 表示經驗或次數常與以下副詞連用：

❶ ever / never

● Have you ever tried bungee jumping? 你有嘗試過高空彈跳嗎？

❷ once / twice / 數字＋times

- **I have been to London for dozens of times, so I could almost recognize every lane in the city.**
  我去過倫敦幾十次了，所以我幾乎可以認出城市裡的每個巷弄。

❸ How long...? / How many times...?

- **How long have you lived in Taipei?** 你住在台北多久了？

3. 「have been to...」和「have gone to...」的區別

❶ 表經驗：**My father has been to the United States.**
我爸爸有去過美國。

❷ 表現在狀況：**My father has gone to the United States.**
我爸爸去美國了。

注意要點

表示「由過去延續到現在」的動作、狀態，常與以下副詞（片語）連用：S + have/ has + V-p.p. 表示發生經驗、持續狀態、完成事件、最後結果
❶ 次數：once/two times
❷ 點／段：since＋時間點；for＋時間段
❸ 最近：recently/lately/of late
❹ 介系詞：in/for/over/during/throughout the last/past＋時間N
❺ 到目前：so far/thus for/as yet / up to now/up to the present time

二、現在完成進行式

句型要點：現在完成式 S+ have + V-p.p. +現在進行式 S + be + V-ing
= 現在完成進行式 S+ have been + V-ing

- 奧利佛已經當16年主廚了。
→Oliver has worked as a chef for 16 years.（→現在可能結束）
→Oliver has been working as a chef for 16 years.（→未來仍會進行）

- 我的父母在市中心住了一輩子。

→My parents have lived in the downtown area all their lives.
（→仍然活著）

→My parents lived in the downtown all their lives.（→已經過世）

- Cockroaches have existed（生存）on the earth for more than two hundred million years.（→for＋一段時間 = 從何時開始）
蟑螂已經在地球上生存了超過兩億年了。

- People's passion（熱情）for egg tarts has decreased（減少）in the past few years.（→in＋一段時間 = 某段時間內）
人們對蛋塔的熱情在過去幾年內已經減少了。

Test 快來即時測驗自己的學習成果吧！

( ) 1. Gary _____ dinner for us, so we don't need to prepare more food.

(A) cook (B) cooking (C) has been cooking (D) has cooked

( ) 2. Jenny _____ for three hours. It's time for her to take a rest.

(A) study (B) studied (C) have studied (D) has been studying

( ) 3. Betty's parents _____ to the outskirt of the city recently.

(A) moves (B) have been moving (C) have moved (D) has moved

( ) 4. Larry _____ his girlfriend the truth, but she doesn't believe his words.

(A) has told (B) have been telling (C) tell (D) have told

( ) 5. The number of brick-and-motor bookstores _____ in the past few years.

(A) decreasing　　　　(B) have decreased

(C) has decreased　　　(D) decrease

解答：(D) (D) (C) (A) (C)

Part **2** | 過去式

 過去簡單式及過去進行式

一、過去簡單式的使用時機：

　　過去簡單式用以表示過去某個時間所發生的事，通常與明確的過去時間連用。而現在完成式用以表示從過去某一個時間一直到現在為止，動作的完成，通常與不明確的時間連用或沒有時間規定。

1. 常與表示「過去時間」的副詞或片語連用：

　　❶ yesterday/the day before yesterday/one day/formerly/previously/this morning/in the past

　　❷ 時間＋ago

　　❸ last＋時間

- **In the past, people in the town got around by bike.**
  過去，這個鎮上的人都騎腳踏車到處走。

- **Michael arrived at the airport about an hour ago.**
  麥可大約在一個小時以前到達機場。

- **My parents bought me a box of medical face masks for the flu season.**
  我父母因為流感季節而買了一盒醫療用口罩給我。

2. 表示過去的習慣：used to＋原形動詞

- **He used to check his email as soon as he entered the office.**
  他以前習慣一進辦公室就收電子郵件。

- **My aunt used to work at a textile factory.**
  我阿姨以前在紡織廠工作。

3. 表示過去的動作、史實、或狀態：

● Cars became widely available in the early twentieth century.
汽車在二十世紀初被廣為使用。

二、過去進行式（was/were＋V-ing）的使用時機：

1. 表示「過去某時正在進行」的動作。

● He was repairing the washing machine at three o'clock this afternoon.
他今天下午三點的時候正在修理洗衣機。

● Thomas and Jack were having a meeting with the client one hour ago.
湯瑪士和傑克一個小時之前正在和客戶開會。

2. 表示「過去正在同時進行」的兩個動作。

● She was phubbing on her smartphone when the bus was approaching the stop.
公車正要進站的時候，她正在滑手機。

● While Jack was livestreaming on Facebook, his pet dog was chewing on his slipper.
傑克在Facebook上直播的時候，他的寵物狗正在咬他的拖鞋。

3. 過去發生的兩個動作

● I was cooking dinner when the doorbell rang.
當我正在煮晚餐時，門鈴響了。

● The hare was struggling to escape from the trap when the hunter approached.
野兔掙扎想逃離陷阱時，獵人接近了。

Test 快來即時測驗自己的學習成果吧！

( ) 1. She used to _____ shopping with her younger sister.
(A) goes (B) go (C) went (D) gone

( ) 2. The villagers evacuated to the shelter when the typhoon
_____.
(A) approach (B) had approached
(C) approaches (D) was approaching

( ) 3. Alexander Graham Bell _____ the telephone in the 19th
century.
(A) invents (B) inventing (C) invented (D) will invent

( ) 4. Kevin _____ a conversation with his supervisor at 10
o'clock this morning.
(A) was having (B) has (C) have (D) have had

( ) 5. Hank _____ food for his customer when we saw him on
the street.
(A) was delivering (B) delivers. (C) deliver (D) have delivered

解答：(B) (D) (C) (A) (A)

過去完成式及過去完成進行式

一、過去完成式及過去完成進行式要點：

Before / When S + have V-p.p. + by the time + S + V-p.t.（先發生）
　　　　　　　　　　　　　　by + 過去時間　　　（後發生）

過去完成式：S + had + Vp.p.
＋過去進行式：S + was / were + V-ing
過去完成進行式：S + had + been + V-ing

二、過去完成式（had＋V-p.p.）的使用時機：

1. 表示「過去某一點時間之前」的動作或狀況。

- Before 1990, computers had been quite common in Taiwan.
  在1990年之前，電腦已經在台灣很普及。
- By the time I entered junior high school, I have learned the computer programming language.
  在我上國中之前，我已經學過電腦程式語言了。

2. 過去的兩個動作，皆發生在過去，一先一後，先發生的動作若早已完成，用過去完成式。

- Finally, Christine realized how much her parents had done for her.
  最後，克麗絲汀明白了她的父母為她做了多少事情。
- I couldn't think of what he had said to make his friend so angry.
  我想不到他說了什麼會讓他的朋友這麼生氣。
- Jack didn't regret what he had done. He would have made the same decision if he could wind back the clock.
  傑克並不後悔他所做的事情。如果他可以讓時光倒流，他會做一樣的決定。

三、過去完成進行式使用時機：

過去完成進行式與過去完成式的異同：

　　同：皆表示動作的發生早於過去式的動作。

　　異：強調動作的連續性。過去完成式表示完成，過去完成進行式表示動作極可能會繼續進行下去。

　　所搭配的時間副詞與過去完成式相同，皆代表動作早於過去，但過去完成進行式只是強調動作的連續性而已。所以過去完成進行式也一樣不能單獨使用，需要過去式與之搭配。

- She had been working out before she purchased the gym membership.
  她在買健身房會員之前就已經有在運動了。

- Lisa had been learning Japanese before she went to Japan for further studies.

  麗莎在去日本進修之前就已經在學習日語了。

- Jenny had been standing at the cashier's desk for the whole day before she finally collapsed.

  珍妮昏倒以前已經在收銀櫃檯站一整天了。

Test 快來即時測驗自己的學習成果吧！

( ) 1. Gary _____ his credit card bill before he received the payment notice.

(A) pays　(B) paying　(C) has paid　(D) had paid

( ) 2. Nick _____ the washing machine when we intended to call him for help.

(A) fixes　(B) is fixing　(C) has fixed　(D) had been fixing

( ) 3. Kevin realized that his colleagues _____ the difficult task for him.

(A) had completed　(B) has completed

(C) completed　(D) completes

( ) 4. Brian _____ videos to online social media when Vincent decided to open his personal weblog.

(A) has uploaded　(B) had been uploading

(C) have uploaded　(D) uploaded

( ) 5. Mr. Wang _____ the traditional handcraft for thirty years when the reporter interviewed him.

(A) makes　(B) make　(C) had been making　(D) have made

解答：(D) (D) (A) (B) (C)

Chapter1 動詞時態與分詞變化

Part 3 | 未來式

 未來簡單式及未來進行式

一、未來簡單式

表達發生在未來的事情,需注意條件句型的用法(見P.160)。

1. 形成方式

❶ 第一人稱+shall /will

- **I always carry a dictionary and look up any words I don't know. Then I will test myself the next time I see those words.**
  我總是帶著字典並查詢我不懂的字,然後我會在下一次看到這些字時做自我測驗。

❷ 第二、三人稱+will

- **The boy will be very upset if he knows the game will be cancelled.**
  如果男孩知道比賽會被取消,他一定會很沮喪。

❸ be going to+VR

- **What are you going to dress up as in the costume party this year?** 你今年的化裝舞會想要扮成誰?

❹ be to+VR

- **I am to meet you at five o'clock this afternoon.**
  我將於下午五點與你會面。

2. 表示未來的動作或狀態:與表示「未來時間」的副詞或片語連用

❶ tomorrow/ the day after tomorrow/ soon/ some day

❷ next+時間

二、未來進行式（will be＋V-ing）的使用時機：

1. 表示「未來某時正在進行」的動作。

- We will be having dinner when you come back.
  你回來的時候，我們應該正在吃晚餐。

- My mother will be cooking dinner when I arrive.
  我到的時候，我媽媽正在煮晚餐。

2. 未來發生的兩個動作。

- I will be grading students' papers when you come tomorrow.
  你明天過來的時候，我正在打學生的成績。

- When you come visiting next summer, I will be preparing my wedding.
  當你明年夏天來訪時，我將在籌備我的婚禮。

Test ——快來即時測驗自己的學習成果吧！

( ) 1. We will be _____ the video games when you go to church.

(A) play　(B) playing　(C) played　(D) plays

( ) 2. After I arrive at the airport, I _____ call you.

(A) will　(B) be　(C) are　(D) were to

( ) 3. The auditorium is to _____ at five o'clock.

(A) closing　(B) being close　(C) be closed　(D) being closing

( ) 4. When you come visiting next Christmas, I _____ planning my trip to Hawaii.

(A)will be　(B)am　(C)was　(D)is going to

( ) 5. According to the weather report, it is _____ to rain tomorrow.

(A)go　(B)goes　(C)went　(D)going

解答：(B) (A) (C) (A) (D)

未來完成式及未來完成進行式

一、未來完成式及未來完成進行式要點

句型要點

> **未來**：S + will + VR
>
> **完成**：S + have + V-p.p. + by the time / before / when + S + V（過去/現在式）By + 未來時間
>
> **未來完成式**：S + will have V-p.p.
>
> **+ 進行式**：S + be V-ing
>
> **= 未來完成進行式**：S + will have been V-ing

二、未來完成式（will have＋V-p.p.）的使用時機：

❶ 表示「未來某點時間將已完成」的動作。

- Next June, I will have studied here for six years.
  到下個六月，我就已經在這裡唸書六年了。

- Your case will have been dealt with when you come here tomorrow afternoon.
  明天下午你來這裡的時候，你的案件就會處理好了。

❷ 未來發生的兩個動作。

- By the time he leaves for New York, he will have become a millionaire.
  當他要前往紐約的時候，他就已經會成為一個百萬富翁了。

- When I travel to Egypt next month, I will have visited twenty countries.
  當我下個月去埃及旅行的時候，我就已經拜訪過二十個國家了。

三、未來完成進行式的使用時間

大致與未來完成式相同，但強調動作的連續及延續性。

- In one more hour, he will have been playing online games for two consecutive days.
  再過一小時，他就連續不間斷地玩網路遊戲兩天了。

 Test 快來即時測驗自己的學習成果吧！

( ) 1. Gary _____ my pen pal for five years by next month.
(A) had been (B) will have been (C) have been (D) is being

( ) 2. By the time you reach the airport, the plan _____.
(A) took off (B) is taking off (C) takes off (D) will have taken off

( ) 3. In five minutes, Mary _____ to her son about the mess in his room for three hours.
(A) have nagged (B) is nagging
(C) will have been nagging (D) would nag

( ) 4. Michael _____ for the company for twenty years by next month.
(A) will have been working (B) had worked
(C) have worked (D) is working

( ) 5. I am sure that Judy _____ her dream by the time we meet her again in New York.
(A) have realized (B) realizes (C) realized (D) will have realized

解答：(B) (D) (C) (A) (D)

024

Part **4** | 分詞的種類

 前位修飾的分詞：V-ing / V-p.p.＋N

現在分詞（V-ing）表主動、進行	過去分詞（V-p.p.）表被動、完成
主動	被動
1. a winding road（蜿蜒的路） 2. visiting scholar（訪問的學者）	1. printed version（印刷版） 2. an imagined country （想像中的國度）
進行	完成或已發生的狀態
1. running water（流動的水/自來水） 2. steaming soup（冒著蒸氣的湯） 3. a developing country （發展中國家）	1. frozen food（冷凍的食物） 2. steamed bun（蒸熟的包子） 3. a developed country （已開發國家）
現在分詞與動名詞很容易混淆，請比較下列兩者	
現在分詞表動作進行的狀態	動名詞表名詞的用途與功能
1. a sleeping cat（正在睡覺的貓） 2. a lifting balloon（正在上升的氣球）	1. a sleeping bag（睡袋） 2. a lifting tool（起重工具）

- Look at those dazzling jewels; they are so beautiful.
  看看那些閃亮的珠寶；真是美麗。（→珠寶使人眩目，為現在分詞）

- Because of my broken arm, I need to see an orthopedist.
  因為我手骨折，我需要去看骨科醫生。（→手是因為外力骨折的，為過去分詞）

- The surprising news changed her mind.
  這令人驚訝的消息使她改變心意。（→消息令人驚訝，為現在分詞）

- The disciplined soldier went all out to complete the assigned mission.
  紀律嚴明的軍人盡全力完成被交代的任務。（→紀律嚴明的，為過去分詞）

- Tourists are reminded to stay away from the grazing cattle.
  遊客被提醒要遠離正在吃草的牛隻。（→正在吃草的牛隻，為現在分詞）
- Maggie threw away the rotten tomatoes in the refrigerator.
  梅姬丟掉冰箱裡那些爛掉的番茄。（→已經腐爛的番茄，為過去分詞）

後位修飾的分詞：N＋V-ing/N＋V-p.p.

1. 定義：動詞後接分詞，當主詞補語，表示主詞的性質或狀態。

2. 分詞當形容詞使用時，可放在所修飾名詞之前或之後，通常短如一個字的分詞放在名詞之前，多字組成的分詞片語則接在名詞之後。

3. 分詞後位修飾可視為由關代所引導的形容詞子句簡化而來，簡化步驟：

❶ **省略關代**：關係代名詞who/which/that是形容子句中的主詞時，將關係代名詞省略。

❷ **動詞改分詞**：將動詞部份改成現在分詞（表主動）或過去分詞（表被動）。

- He threw away a broken computer screen.
  = He threw away the computer screen which was broken.
  他把壞掉的電腦螢幕丟了。

  → He threw away the computer screen (which is) broken by his son.
  他把被他兒子弄壞的電腦螢幕丟了。
  （→省略關代＋beV，保留分詞及分詞後的補語）
- There is smog hovering over the industrial area.
  霧霾籠罩在工業區的上方。（→省略which are）
- Many singers performed on the philanthropic concert hosted by a charity organization.
  許多歌手在那場由慈善機構舉辦的慈善音樂會上表演。
  （→省略which was）
- Laborers working in the factory have to take night shifts every two weeks.
  在這間工廠工作的勞工每兩個星期都要值夜班。（→省略who are）

Test ——快來即時測驗自己的學習成果吧！

( ) 1. There are some stray dogs _____ on this street.

    (A) wanders   (B) wander   (C) wandering   (D) wandered

( ) 2. The newly _____ magazines have been sold out.

    (A) releasing   (B) released   (C) releases   (D) release

( ) 3. The widely _____ news turned out to be a hoax.

    (A) spread   (B) spreading   (C) spreads   (D) to spread

( ) 4. She had problem opening the tightly _____ package.

    (A) sealing   (B) seals   (C) sealed   (D) seal

( ) 5. Peter said some _____ words to the disappointed boy.

    (A) comforted   (B) comforts   (C) comforts   (D) comforting

解答：(C) (B) (A) (C) (D)

複合形容詞I：N/ adj./ adv.＋V-ing

1. 複合形容詞，做形容詞用：分詞可和副詞、形容詞、名詞或介系詞搭配，以連字號連接。

2. 複合形容詞可視為形容詞子句的簡化，形容詞子句中的動詞與所修飾名詞（即先行詞）之間，若為主動關係則用現在分詞，若為被動關係則用過去分詞。

- Young people need the skills to adapt themselves to the fast changing society.（→ the society that is changing fast）
  年輕人需要適應快速變遷的社會的技能。

- For centuries, Christianity has had a far-reaching influence on Western culture.（→influence which reaches far）
  好幾世紀以來，基督教對西方文化產生深遠的影響。

- It is said that gasoline-powered cars produce more pollution than electric cars.（→ the cars that are powered by gasoline）
  據說由石油燃料驅動的車會比電動車製造更多污染。

- **Many people are waiting in line for the freshly-baked egg tarts.**
（→**the egg tarts that are baked freshly**）
很多人排隊買剛出爐的蛋塔。

3. N與V-ing/V-p.p. 搭配的用法，說明如下

	定義：相當於形容詞子句中，**及物動詞與受詞的關係**。(S＋V＋O)→吃人的怪物 **man-eating beast**（beast eats man）
N＋V-ing	範例解說： ❶ an **energy-saving** machine = a machine **which saves** energy 　一台節能的機器 ❷ a **peace-loving** person = a person **that loves peace** 　愛好和平的人 ❸ a **law-abiding** citizen = a citizen **who abides by the law** 　遵守法律的公民 ❹ **flag-raising** ceremony = a ceremony **that raises flags** 　升旗典禮 ❺ a **time-wasting** hobby　浪費時間的嗜好 　a **body-building** food　有助身體成長的食物 　a **heart-breaking** story　令人心碎的故事

4. adv. 與V-ing/V-p.p. 搭配的用法，說明如下：

	定義：等於形容詞子句中，**不及物動詞與副詞的關係**。(S＋V＋adv.) →深遠的影響 **far-reaching** influence（influence reaches far）
adv.＋V-ing	範例解說： ❶ a **hard-working** man = a man **who works hard** 　認真工作的男人 ❷ a **slowly-flowing** river = a river **that flows slowly** 　流速緩慢的河 ❸ a **never-ending** quarrel = a quarrel **which never ends** 　永不停止的爭吵

5. adj. 與V-ing/V-p.p. 搭配的用法，說明如下：

adj.＋V-ing	**定義：**相當於形容詞子句中，**動詞**與**形容詞**（當主詞補語用）的關係，此類動詞常為連綴動詞，如look, taste, smell。(S＋V＋adj.)→難聽的語言 **harsh-sounding** language（language sounds harsh） **範例解說：** ❶ **stinky-smelling** tofu = tofu **that smells stinky** 　聞起來很臭的豆腐 ❷ a **good-looking** guy = a guy **who looks good** 　很好看的男生 ❸ a **lovely-looking** girl = a girl **who looks lovely** 　很好看的女生 ❹ a **sweet-smelling** flower = a flower **which smells sweet** 　聞起來很香的花 ❺ an **ill-fitting** clothes = a clothes **that fits ill** 　不合身的衣服

- Under the trend of environmental movements, energy-saving appliances are getting more and more popular.

  （→**appliances that save energy**，為N＋V-ing結構）
  在環保運動的趨勢下，節能家電愈來愈受歡迎。

- We are all living in this ever-changing world.

  （→**world ever changes**，為adv.＋V-ing結構）
  我們生活在這個不斷改變的世界裡。

- My father prefers bitter-tasting coffee.

  （→**coffee that tastes bitter**，為adj.＋V-ing結構）
  我父親偏愛苦的咖啡。

 **複合形容詞II：N/adj./adv.＋V-p.p.**

1. N與V-p.p. 搭配的用法，說明如下：

N＋V-p.p.	**定義**：相當於形容詞子句中，被動語態裡**S＋V-p.p.**或**O＋V-p.p.**的關係。(S＋be動詞＋V-p.p.＋by/with/like/to＋O)→因飢餓而瘦弱的男孩 **hunger-weakened** boy (a boy is weakened by hunger)
	範例解說： ❶ a **heart-broken** girl = a girl **whose heart is broken**　心碎的女孩 ❷ **smoking-related** death = death **which is related to smoking**　和吸菸有關的死亡 ❸ a **drought-stricken** area = an area th**at is stricken by drought**　被乾旱侵襲的國家 ❹ a **poverty-stricken** family = a family **which is stricken by poverty**　被貧窮侵襲的家庭

2. adj.與V-p.p.搭配的用法，說明如下：

adj.＋V-p.p.	**定義**：相當於形容詞子句中，**及物動詞與形容詞**（當受詞補語用）的關係。(S＋V＋O＋adj.或S＋be動詞＋V-p.p.＋adj.)→染成金色的頭髮 **blond-dyed** hair (hair is dyed blond)
	範例解說： ❶ **ready-made** clothes = clothes **that are made ready**　現成的衣服 ❷ a **ready-made** dress = a dress **which is made ready**　現成的洋裝 ❸ a **green-painted** wall = a wall **which is painted green**　漆成綠色的牆壁

3. adv.與V-p.p.搭配的用法,說明如下:

adj.＋V-p.p.	**定義**:相當於形容詞子句中,**及物動詞**與**副詞**的關係。(S＋V＋O＋adv.或S＋be動詞＋V-p.p.＋adv.) →精雕細琢的句子 **carefully-crafted** sentence (a sentence is crafted carefully) **範例解說:** ❶ a **carefully-designed** machine = a machine **which is carefully designed** 　精心設計的機器 ❷ a **never-taken** path = a path **that is never taken** 　沒有走過的路 ❸ a **well-dressed** man = a man **who is dressed well** 　打扮得很好看的男人

4. 其他用法

V-p.p.＋prep	**定義:** 相當於形容詞子句中,**動詞**與**介系詞/介副詞**的關係。 (S＋V＋O＋prep.) **範例解說:** ❶ a computer with a **built-in** microphone 　= a microphone **which is build in** the computer 　內建麥克風的電腦 ❷ a **built-up** area = an area **that is built up** 　建築物密集的地區 ❸ a **burnt-out** house = a house **that is burnt out** 　被燒空的房子

- She wore a self-designed wedding gown at her wedding. （→a wedding gown which was designed by herself，為N＋V-p.p.結構）
  她在婚禮上穿著自己設計的婚紗禮服。

- The pink colored pencils have been sold out.

  （→the pencils which were colored pink，為adj.＋V-p.p.結構）
  被染成粉紅色的鉛筆已經賣光了。

- We were amazed by the beautifully-decorated hall.

  （→the hall which is decorated beautifully，為adv.＋V-p.p.結構）
  我們為了這個裝飾得很美的大廳感到驚訝。

- He has been working on the report for two days and he looks worn-out now.

  （→he has worn himself out，為V-p.p.＋prep結構）
  他已經做這個報告做了兩天，現在他看起來精疲力竭。

- It's not easy to work with a hot-tempered supervisor.

  （→a supervisor with hot temper，為adj.＋N-ed結構）
  和一位脾氣暴躁的上司一起工作很不容易。

延伸學習

❶ 副詞well通常搭配V-p.p.形成複合形容詞

well-educated 受良好教育的	**well-known** 知名的
well-behaved 行為端正的	**well-prepared** 準備充分的
well-built 體格健壯的	**well-dressed** 穿著入時的

❷ 複合形容詞adv.＋V-p.p.中，若搭配字尾為-ly的副詞時，-ly副詞和V-p.p.間的連字號可省略

newly-fallen snow 新下的雪

a beautifully performed song 演唱優美的歌曲

an efficiently operated company 經營有效率的公司

Test 快來即時測驗自己的學習成果吧！

( ) 1. The _____ news about coronavirus caused panic among people.
(A) horrifying
(B) horrified
(C) horrifies
(D) horrify

( ) 2. We have been making improvement in this program, and now it is a _____ tool for computer users.
(A) good-developing
(B) well-developing
(C) good-developed
(D) well-developed

( ) 3. A _____ beagle will weigh about 22 to 24 pounds.
(A) fully-growing
(B) fully-grow
(C) full-growing
(D) fully-grown

( ) 4. The outfit store only sells _____ dresses.
(A) readily-making
(B) ready-making
(C) ready-made
(D) readily-made

( ) 5. Negotiating with the client is a _____ task.
(A) time-consuming
(B) time-consumed
(C) consuming-time
(D) consumed-time

 情緒形容詞

1. 常見用來表達情緒的形容詞，用過去分詞和現在分詞會有不同的意思。

表自身的身心感受，如：驚訝、高興、滿意、失望、疲倦等的動詞概念，通常用**過去分詞V-p.p.**。	外界事物令人產生之各種身心感受，如令人驚訝、令人高興、令人滿意、令人厭倦、令人疲倦等的動詞概念，通常用**現在分詞V-ing**。
某人「感到……的」、某物「顯露出內心……感到……的」	某事物或某人「令人覺得……的」、「使人感到……的」
1. a **surprised** expression 　一個吃驚的表情	1. a **surprising** result 　令人吃驚的結果
2. an **interested** audience 　一個有興趣的聽眾	2. an **interesting** lecture 　一場有趣的演說
(be) obliged 感激的	(be) obliging 樂於助人的
(be) perplexed 困惑的	(be) perplexing 令人費解的
(be) confused 感到疑惑的	(be) confusing 令人困惑的
(be) puzzled 困惑的	(be) puzzling 令人不解的
(be) embarrassed 感到困窘的	(be) embarrassing 令人尷尬的
(be) annoyed 惱怒的	(be) annoying 惱人的
(be) disgusted 作嘔的	(be) disgusting 令人作嘔的
(be) discouraged 洩氣的	(be) discouraging 令人沮喪的
(be) disappointed 失望的	(be) disappointing 令人失望的
(be) amused 被逗樂的	(be) amusing 引人發笑的
(be) delighted 感到開心的	(be) delighting 令人開心的
(be) astonished 吃驚的	(be) astonishing 令人驚訝的
(be) horrified 恐懼的	(be) horrifying 令人驚駭的
(be) terrified 害怕的	(be) terrifying 恐怖的
(be) exhausted 筋疲力竭的	(be) exhausting 使人筋疲力盡的
(be) satisfied 滿意的	(be) satisfying 令人滿意的
(be) tired 疲累的	(be) tiring 累人的
(be) pleased 歡喜的	(be) pleasing 令人愉快的
(be) amazed 驚奇的	(be) amazing 令人吃驚的
(be) excited 興奮的	(be) exciting 令人激動的
(be) irritated 被惹惱的	(be) irritating 引人惱怒的

2. 英文中有些動詞常以被動形式出現，但並未帶有被動的意思，也特別注意其後所接的介系詞。

(be) related **to** 與……相關的	(be) divided (**into**) 被分成……
(be) associated **with** 與……有關聯的	(be) connected **with** 與……相連結的
(be) suited **for** 與……相稱的	(be) obliged **to** 對……感激的
(be) experienced **in** 在……方面有經驗的	(be) involved **in** 牽涉……其中
(be) shaped **with** 被劃分……	(be) inclined **to** 傾向於……
(be) seated **in** 坐在……	(be) dressed **in** 著裝
(be) bounded **for** 注定要……	(be) mistaken **for** 被誤認為……
(be) qualified **for** 合乎標準	(be) addicted **to** 沉溺在……
(be) acquainted **with** 熟習……	(be) destined **to** 注定要……
(be) prepared **for** 為……作準備	(be) concerned **about** 關於……
(be) absorbed **in** 全神貫注於……	(be) determined **to** 決心要……
(be) engaged **in** 從事……	(be) made (up) **of** 由……製成
(be) dedicated **to** 致力於……	(be) composed **of** 由……所組成
(be) devoted **to** 致力於……	(be) well-known **for/as** 以……聞名
(be) accustomed **to** 習慣於……	(be) noted **for/as** 以……著名
(be) used **to** 習慣於……	(be) celebrated **for/as** 慶祝……
(be) situated **in/at** 座落於……	(be) based **on** 以……為基礎
(be) opposed **to** 反對……	(be) married **to** 嫁娶……
(be) supposed **to** 應該……	(be) convinced **of** 為……所信服
	(be) located **in/at** 座落於……
	(be) exposed **to** 暴露在……

- **The boy is very excited about the family trip this weekend.**
  男孩對於週末的家庭旅行感到非常興奮。

- **Helen is married to the man she met on a blind date last year.**
  海倫和一個去年在相親時認識的男子結婚。

- **Gary was exhausted after attending a two-day conference.**
  蓋瑞參加完兩天的研討會之後感到精疲力竭。
- **Nancy was absorbed in the sci-fi novel.**
  南茜專注在閱讀這本科幻小說。
- **Betty turned off the TV because she was tired of watching sensational gossip of the celebrities.**
  貝蒂關掉電視，因為她對於看名人的八卦感到很厭倦。

Test 快來即時測驗自己的學習成果吧！

( ) 1. David's words were quite _____. We didn't know what exactly he meant.
   (A) confused   (B) confusing   (C) confuse   (D) confuses

( ) 2. I couldn't say anything because I was _____ by his sudden action.
   (A) terrifying   (B) terrify   (C) terrified   (D) terrifies

( ) 3. She looked _____ about this concept. We should give some more examples for her.
   (A) perplexing   (B) perplexed   (C) perplexes   (D) perplex

( ) 4. My teacher wrote some _____ words to me, which motivated me to keep pursuing my goal.
   (A) encouraging   (B) encouraged
   (C) disappointed   (D) disappoints

( ) 5. The _____ audience gave the comedian a round of applause.
   (A) amuses   (B) amuse   (C) amusing   (D) amused

解答：(B) (C) (B) (A) (D)

Part 5 │ 分詞的補語用法

 ## 1. 主詞補語用法：S＋V＋SC

這些動詞後面接分詞，當主詞補語用，表示主詞的性質或狀態。主動用現在分詞，被動用過去分詞。

❶ be動詞

❷ 保持動詞: remain/keep/maintain

❸ 似乎動詞: seem/appear

❹ 變成動詞: become/go/turn/get/grow

❺ 來去動詞: go/come/escape

❻ 站坐動詞: stand/sit/lie

這些動詞後面除了接分詞之外，也可以接形容詞當主詞補語，其他動詞也有類似用法。

● When he realized that his wallet was stolen, he became stunned.

當他發現自己的錢包不見了，他變得不知所措。

● The kid refused to remain seated at the dinner table.

小孩拒絕靜靜坐在桌子上吃晚餐。

● The suspect seemed irritated when the police asked him some questions.

嫌疑犯在警察問他問題時似乎很生氣。

( ) 1. He kept _____ so as not to wake up the sleeping baby.
   (A) tiptoed   (B) tiptoeing   (C) tiptoes   (D) tiptoe

( ) 2. She appeared _____ when she got the small prize at the
   year-end party.
   (A) disappoints (B) disappointing (C) disappointed (D) disappoint

( ) 3. Michael remained _____ about his supervisor's instruction.
   (A) confused   (B) confusing   (C) confuse   (D) confusion

( ) 4. Larry remained _____ about his parents' health condition.
   (A) concern   (B) concerns   (C) concerned   (D) concerning

( ) 5. He escaped _____ from the concentration camp.
   (A) harming   (B) harms   (C) unharmed   (D) harm

解答：(B) (C) (A) (C) (C)

2. 表達「位於」的句型

1. 用於表示某物位於某地，句型即為S＋V＋SC，有下列動詞及固定用法。

❶ locate/situate/seat 用被動

　句型：be located/situated/seated＋介系詞＋某地

❷ sit/stand/lie/rest 用主動

　句型：sit/stand/lie/rest＋介系詞＋某地

❸ nestle指位於群山之間，若隱若現的位置，用主動或被動都可以。

2. 這些表示位置的動詞，要搭配適當的介系詞。

• **The luxurious hotel lies by the riverside.**
　這間豪華的旅館位於河畔。

- **The product he asked for is situated on the top shelf.**
  他要求的商品放在架子的最上層。
- **His deli was located near the main entrance of the train station.**
  他的書報攤位於靠近火車站的大門口。
- **The cottage is nestled in (nestles) the forest in the mountain.**
  那個偏遠的村落依偎在連綿的群山之間。
- **The gasoline station is located in (locates) the center of the town.**
  那個加油站坐落於市鎮的中心。
- **The GPS in your car can help us locate our destination.**
  你車上的GPS可以幫我們定位目的地。

延伸學習

lie in 除了表是「位於」以外，也可以表示「在於」，等於consist in。

- **Happiness consists in contentment.**
  知足常樂。
- **His success lies in his confidence and eloquence that makes the projects he promotes more convincing.**
  他的成功在於他的信心和流利的口條，使得他推動的計畫更有說服力。

( ) 1. The library is _____ next to the community service center.

(A) locates   (B) located   (C) locating   (D) locate

( ) 2. Her mansion _____ in the middle of the woods.

(A) situates   (B) have situated   (C) to situate   (D) is situating

( ) 3. The headquarter of the company _____ in the most prosperous district of the city.

(A) locate   (B) lie in   (C) situate   (D) stands

( ) 4. The beautiful castle _____ the edge of a cliff.

(A) lies in   (B) locates   (C) situates   (D) located

( ) 5. The monument of the martyr _____ in a park near his hometown.

(A) lie   (B) rests   (C) situate   (D) locate

解答：(B) (A) (D) (A) (B)

3. 動詞find/keep/catch/leave＋O＋OC

1. 口訣：抓發保留 catch/find/keep/leave

2. catch（撞見、當場逮到）、**find**（發現）、**keep**（使……保持某種狀態）、**leave**（使……處於某種狀態）後的受詞補語，若為現在分詞**V-ing**，則表動詞與受詞間的主動關係，過去分詞**V-p.p.**則表被動關係。

3. 除了分詞之外，受詞補語也可以是形容詞片語、介係詞片語或介副詞。

• **The clerk caught the shoplifter put the goods into his bag sneakily.**

店員當場捉到扒手偷偷將商品放進袋子裡。

- When James was about to pay, he found his credit card gone.
  詹姆士要付錢的時候，發現他的信用卡不見了。
- Sometimes it is better to leave the words unsaid.
  有時候有些話不說出口比較好。

Test 快來即時測驗自己的學習成果吧！

( ) 1. Linda was found _____ into the classroom while the teacher was doing the roll call.

(A) sneaked   (B) sneaking   (C) sneaks   (D) sneak

( ) 2. Parents should never leave their children _____ on the street.

(A) wandered   (B) wanders   (C) wandering   (D) wonder

( ) 3. The school wants to keep the scandal _____, so teachers have been told not to reveal any details to the reporters.

(A) public   (B) publicize   (C) publicly   (D) unpublished

( ) 4. The police kept the vital evidence _____ from the public.

(A) concealed   (B) conceal   (C) concealing   (D) to conceal

( ) 5. We should keep the vulnerable flower _____.

(A) to harm   (B) harming   (C) unharmed   (D) harm

解答：(B) (C) (D) (A) (C)

 **4. 感官動詞的用法**

1. 感官動詞作及物動詞用時，受詞與補語之間的關係為主動時，補語可用原形動詞（表示事實或過程），或是現在分詞 **V-ing**（表示動作正在進行）。受詞與補語的關係為被動時，補語要用過去分詞**V-p.p.**。

2. 感官動詞列表

❶ 看：see/watch/look at

❷ 聽：hear/listen to

❸ 聞：smell

❹ 嘗：taste

❺ 感：feel/notice/observe

- <u>I felt the wind blowing through my hair.</u>
  S V　　O　　　　C
  我感覺到風吹過我的頭髮。

- I like to listen to people sharing their life experience.
  我喜歡傾聽人們分享他們的生命經驗。

  感官動詞為被動時，原本為原形動詞的受詞補語要改成to＋V。

  ❶ 主動式：S＋see/hear/feel/smell/taste＋O＋V

  ❷ 被動式：S＋be seen/heard/felt/smelled＋to＋V(＋ by＋O)

- I heard her mumbling the excuses for being late.
  我聽到她含糊不清地說著遲到的藉口。

Test 快來即時測驗自己的學習成果吧！

( ) 1. She was seen _____ through the book with interest.
(A) to browse　(B) browse　　(C) browsing　(D) browsed

( ) 2. If your mom sees you _____ on your smartphone again, she will be very angry.
(A) phubbing　(B) to phub　　(C) phubbed　(D) phubs

( ) 3. We smelled something _____ when we entered the kitchen.
(A) burns　　(B) to burn　　(C) burning　(D) is burnt

( ) 4. She was seen _____ the koalas trapped in the wild fire.
(A) rescuing　(B) rescue　　(C) rescued　(D) to rescue

( ) 5. Some people said that they felt the ground _____ after the gas explosion.
(A) to shake　(B) shaken　　(C) shakes　(D) shaking

解答：(A) (A) (C) (D) (D)

Note

Part 6 | 分詞構句

 1. 一般分詞構句簡化（前後子句主詞相同時）

1. 副詞子句改為分詞構句，首先必須先將引導副詞子句的連接詞去掉。再者，若副詞子句的主詞與主要子句的主詞相同時，則將副詞子句的主詞去掉；如不相同則保留。最後，將動詞（包括**be**動詞）改為現在分詞，其餘照抄。

● After the sun had set, we arrived at our destination.

= After the sun had → having set, we arrived at the station.

= The sun having set, we arrived at our destination.
太陽下山後，我們抵達了目的地。（→主詞不同予以保留）

2. 副詞子句中如是進行式，則須把**be**動詞去掉才行。

● When he was dining at the exotic restaurant, he met an old friend.
= Dining at the exotic restaurant, he met an old friend.
他在異國風餐廳用餐的時候，遇見一位老朋友。

3. 從屬子句中的動詞若是**be**動詞則須變為**being**並判斷是否省略。

● As James was exhilarated about the news, he informed his family immediately.

= Being exhilarated about the news, James informed his family immediately.

= Exhilarated about the news, James informed his family immediately.
詹姆士為這個消息感到興高采烈，立刻就通知他的家人。

4. 分詞為**being**和**having been**時，可省略。

- As he has been scolded too much, he becomes somewhat intimidated.

  = (Having been) scolded too much, he becomes somewhat intimidated.

  他因為受到過份的責備，而變得有些膽怯。

5. 原副詞子句中有否定詞，則將否定詞放在分詞前形成分詞構句。

- Because the guard didn't know who the women was, he stopped her.

  = Not knowing who the woman was, the guard stopped her.

  因為不知道那位女性是誰，警衛攔住了她。

- Because Joyce was not satisfied with my report, she asked me to revise it.

  = Not being satisfied with my report, Joyce asked me to revise it.

  因為喬伊斯對我的報告不滿意，便叫我重改一次。

6. 分詞構句所顯示的連接詞意思，從句子的前後關係來判斷，但為了使其意義明確，方有將連接詞置於分詞之前面。

- While fighting in Iraq, he was taken prisoner.

  在伊拉克作戰時，他被俘了。

7. 分詞構句依其意義可分為：

❶ 表時間（由when, while, as soon as, as, after等引導的副詞子句）

- When he roamed in the city, he saw a internet celebrity having a fan meeting.

  當他在街上散步時，看到一個網紅在辦粉絲見面會。

❷ 表原因、理由（由as, because, since等引導的副詞子句）

- Because I was exhausted, I didn't go to the party yesterday.

  = Being exhausted, I didn't go to the party yesterday.

  因為精疲力盡，我昨天沒去參加派對。

❸ 表條件：（由if引導的副詞子句）

- If you speak of the wolf, you will see his tail

  = Speaking of the wolf, you will see his tail.

  【諺】說曹操，曹操到。

❹ 表讓步：（though等為引導的副詞子句）

- Though she was not feeling very well, she still attended the meeting.

  = Not feeling very well, she still attended the meeting.

  雖然身體不太舒服，她還是參加了這場會議。

❺ 表附帶狀況：（由and引導的子句）

- His grandmother passed away, and she left a great amount of fortune.

  = His grandmother passed away, leaving a great amount of fortune.

  他的祖母去世了，留下很大一筆財富。

8. 分詞構句的位置，可置於句首、句中（主詞之後）、句尾，但都要用逗點隔開。

- Arguing for the giveaways at the counter, the shopper caught a lot of attention.

  = The shopper, arguing for the giveaways at the counter, caught a lot of attention.

  = The shopper argued for giveaways at the counter, catching a lot of attention.

  購物者在櫃檯吵著要贈品，引起許多人注意。

- Tom forgot his line for the stage play, feeling embarrassed.

  = Forgetting his line for the stage play, Tom felt embarrassed.

  因為忘記了舞台劇的台詞，湯姆感到很尷尬。

- When Jane saw the Korean actor in person, she could feel her heart racing.

  = Seeing the Korean actor in person, Jane could feel her heart racing.

  當珍看到那個韓國演員本人的時候，她感覺自己心跳得很快。

- As it was fine, I went skateboarding with my brother.

  = The weather being fine, I went skateboarding with my brother

  因為天氣好，所以我和弟弟去玩滑板。

- After they rehearsed for the stage play for the whole day, the actors were exhausted.

  = Rehearsing for the stage play for the whole day, the actors were exhausted.

  排練舞台劇一整天之後，演員都累垮了。

- I was working on my report, and my sister was chatting with her friend on the phone.

  = I was working on my report, my sister chatting with her friend on the phone.

  我在做報告，而我妹妹在跟朋友講電話。

9. 若分詞構句由being或having been引導時，常常會省略being或having been，而形成形容詞或名詞引導的句子。

- The boy was unnoticed, and he took some commodities from the store without paying any money.

  = Unnoticed, the boy took some commodities from the store without paying any money.

  沒人注意到他，這個男孩就從商店拿走一些商品而不付任何錢。

- He is a member of the royal family, and he has to be cautious about his words and deeds.

  = A member of the royal family, he has to be cautious about his words and deeds.

  身為皇室成員，他必須謹言慎行。

10. 以分詞構句描述過去事件時，若兩個動作的發生有先後之分，先發生的動作用Having＋V-p.p.表示，亦可保留表時間之連接詞，以釐清兩動詞的相對先後關係。

- Having gotten his supervisor's permission, he started to carry out the plan. (O)
- After getting his supervisor's permission, he started to carry out the plan. (O)
- Getting his supervisor's permission, he started to carry out the plan. (X)

  獲得上司的允許之後，他開始實踐這項計畫。

( ) 1. _____ about the field trip, Tom started to prepare his backpack really early.

(A) He is excited   (B) Being excited

(C) Exciting   (D) To excite

( ) 2. _____ what to say, Joe decided to remain silent.

(A) He doesn't know   (B) He not know

(C) He knows   (D) Not knowing

( ) 3. _____ every day, she finally loses some weight.

(A) Having excised   (B) Exercising   (C) To exercise   (D) Exercised

( ) 4. The weather _____, they went on hiking together.

(A) being fine   (B) is fine   (C) has been   (D) to be

( ) 5. _____ to the interviewer, the singer used some gestures to stress her idea.

(A) She talks   (B) To talk   (C) While talking   (D) She is talking

解答：(B) (D) (B) (A) (C)

2. 獨立分詞構句 S1＋V-ing/V-p.p., S2＋V...

1. 分詞構句的主詞與主要句子的主詞不同時，必須將主詞保留，形成獨立分詞構句。此外，在簡化的步驟與用法上均與分詞構句相同。簡化步驟如下：

❶ 先判斷主詞：前後兩子句的主詞不同，將主詞保留。

❷ 刪去連接詞：需要時可將連接詞保留，使語意明確。

❸ 動詞改分詞：將連接詞所引導的子句中的動詞改成分詞，主動關係用現在分詞，被動關係用過去分詞。

• If time permits, we will send refreshments to our colleagues who are working overtime.

= Time permitting, we will send refreshments to our colleagues who are working overtime.

如果時間許可，我們將會送一些點心去給在加班的同事。

2. 分詞構句中的意思上的主詞必須和主要句子中的主詞一致，及分詞結構應與主詞有關，否則務必在分詞前加上其意思上的主語，亦即要使用「獨立分詞構句」，以免寫出如下列例句般錯誤而語意不合邏輯的句子來。

• Kept in the cage, the children are not frightened of the lion. X
  此句意思是孩子們被關在籠子裡。

• The lion kept in the cage, the children are not frightened of it. O
  此句意思為獅子被關在籠子裡。

• There were no restaurants open during the holiday, so we decided to eat at home.

  = There being no restaurants open during the holiday, we decided to eat at home.
  假日沒有餐館有開，我們決定在家吃飯。

• Because Kevin speaks more than ten languages, many people asked him about the tips of learning a new language.

  = Speaking more than ten languages, many people ask Kevin about the tips of learning a new language.
  因為凱文會說超過十種語言，許多人就問他學習新語言的秘訣。

• When the clock stroke five, we then called it a day.

  = The clock striking five, we then called it a day.
  當時鐘敲五下時，我們就下班了。

• She was stumbling along the street, and tears rolled down her cheeks.

  = She was stumbling along the street, tears rolling down her cheeks.
  她沿著街道跌跌撞撞走著，眼淚流下臉頰。

表「連續或附帶狀態」的獨立分構，可與with＋O＋OC的句型互換。

- She walked out and her skirt blew up.
= She walked out, her skirt blowing up.
= She walked out with her skirt blowing up.
  她走出來，裙擺飛揚。

Test ─ 快來即時測驗自己的學習成果吧！

( ) 1. She smiled, _____ in her eyes.

    (A) her tears glittering   (B) her tears glittered

    (C) with her tears glitter   (D) her tears glitter

( ) 2. _____, we will go hiking in the woods.

    (A) The weather permits   (B) Weather permitting

    (C) If the weather permit   (D) With the weather permitting

( ) 3. Joe _____ a highly successful career, many people view him as a model.

    (A) has   (B) is having   (C) was having   (D) having

( ) 4. _____ insufficient water resource, people in the village have poor hygiene.

    (A) They had   (B) Without   (C) There being   (D) Because of

( ) 5. The superstar walking down the aisle, her body guard _____ the fans away from her.

    (A) stopped   (B) stopping   (C) to stop   (D) are stopping

解答：(A) (B) (D) (C) (B)

3. with＋O＋OC

1. with表伴隨主要動作所發生的動作、狀態或提供細節的描述。

2. 此句型以分詞作為受詞補語，補充說明受詞的狀態，用現在分詞表示動詞與受詞間的主動關係，過去分詞則表示被動關係。

3. 如果從屬子句和主要子句主詞不同而兩動作發生於同時，可用(S＋V..., with＋O＋OC)的附帶狀態句型，with有時亦可省略。

- The mother duck walked ahead and three ducklings followed her closely.

  = The mother duck walked ahead, with her three ducklings following her closely.

  那母鴨走在前頭，三隻小鴨緊跟在後。

- Sally danced clumsily, and her foot stumbled her partner.

  = Sally danced clumsily with her foot stumbling her partner.

  莎莉笨拙地跳著舞，腳去絆到舞伴。

- Jason sent me a package and a card was attached to it.

  = Jason sent me a package with a card attached to it.

  傑森寄了一封夾帶卡片的包裹給我。

- Mr. Robinson sat reading a magazine on the sofa and his legs were crossed.

  = Mr. Robinson sat reading a magazine on the sofa with his legs crossed.

  羅賓森先生翹著二郎腿，坐在沙發上看雜誌。

　　句型的OC是現在分詞或過去分詞之外，也可以是形容詞片語、介系詞片語或介副詞、不定詞片語。

- I can't shake with you with my hands full.（→OC為adj.）

  我手上有很多東西無法與你握手。

- Maggie entered the room with bag of groceries in her hands.（→OC為介系詞片語）

  梅姬走進房間，手裡拿著一袋雜貨。

- The apple pie dropped to the floor with the upside down.

（→OC為介系詞／副詞）

蘋果派正面朝下掉到地板上。

- He was overwhelmed with so many deadlines to meet.

（→OC為不定詞片語）

他有多項得在規定日期之前完成的工作，為此感到快要崩潰。

Test ——快來即時測驗自己的學習成果吧！

( ) 1. She answered 'No' with her head _____.

    (A) shaking   (B) to shake   (C) shakes   (D) have shaken

( ) 2. Shoppers have more choices with the number of malls _____.

    (A) increased   (B) will increase   (C) increases   (D) increasing

( ) 3. She felt stressed out with so many tasks _____.

    (A) completed   (B) to complete   (C) completing   (D) completes

( ) 4. Kelly is confident about the accuracy of the report with all her team members _____ on it.

    (A) checks   (B) check   (C) to check   (D) having checked

( ) 5. Susan couldn't walk with the wire of the microphone _____ on her feet.

    (A) tangling   (B) to tangle   (C) tangled   (D) tangles

解答：(A) (D) (D) (B) (C)

4. 分詞慣用語

此類分詞慣用語又稱為「無人稱獨立分詞片語」。因其意思上的主詞為一般人，如we、you、one、they等，故通常將該主詞省略無須寫出，具獨立分詞構句的結構。常見的分詞慣用語有：

(1) 由於	owing to + N
(2) 根據…	based on / upon + N
(3) 關於…	concerning / regarding / respecting + N
(4) 從…來判斷	judging from + N
(5) 和…相較之下	compared with + N
(6) 談到、提到	speaking of + N
(7) 因為、鑑於	seeing that + S + V
(8) 倘若、假設	provided / providing / supposing that S+V
(9) 考慮到	considering + N / that + S + V
(10) 如果考慮到	given N / that + S+V
(11) 根據…所說/而定	according to + N
(12) 說來…ly	speaking,
（大致說來）	roughly speaking,
（廣泛說來）	broadly speaking,
（法律上說來）	legally speaking,

（坦白説來）	frankly speaking,
（正確説來）	correctly speaking,
（嚴格説來）	strictly speaking,
（一般説來）	generally speaking,
（比較上説來）	comparatively speaking,

- **Judging from her cold attitude, she is probably against the project.** 從她冷淡的態度來看，她應該是反對這個計畫。

- **Speaking of coronavirus, more and more scientists warn the public of its threats and possible transmission.**
説到冠狀病毒，越來越多科學家警告大家它的威脅和傳染的可能。

- **Considering that your plan couldn't work, what would you do?**
要是你的計畫無法實行，你怎麼辦？

- **Given that they couldn't have stable supply of raw material, they could only deliver half of the ordered goods this week.**
考慮到原物料的供給不穩定，他們這星期只能供給一半的貨物。

- **Roughly speaking, entrepreneurs spend more time on reading per week.** 大致上來説，企業家每週會花更多的時間閱讀。

Note

Test 快來即時測驗自己的學習成果吧！

( ) 1. _____, people living in the city enjoy more resources than people in the rural area.
(A) Generally speaking
(B) Given that
(C) Speaking strictly
(D) Speaking legally

( ) 2. _____, women's suffrage (投票權) is protected all over the nation.
(A) Comparatively
(B) Legally speaking
(C) Concerning
(D) Owing to

( ) 3. _____ there could be a stock market crash, investors started to feel anxious.
(A) Provided
(B) Regarding
(C) Correctly speaking
(D) Seeing that

( ) 4. _____ her graceful manner, she is probably a well-educated lady.
(A) Roughly speakin
(B) Speaking of
(C) Judging from
(D) Compared with

( ) 5. _____ the housing marker, Mike is the expert.
(A) Speaking of
(B) According to
(C) Seeing that
(D) Compared with

解答：(A) (B) (D) (C) (A)

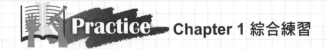

( ) 1. Linda _____ in the gym once a week.
    (A) goes exercising   (B) exercising
    (C) going exercising   (D) go exercising

( ) 2. Joe _____ in the culinary school in Europe three years ago.
    (A) studies   (B) is studying
    (C) has studied   (D) studied

( ) 3. So far, Kevin _____ over twenty countries around the world.
    (A) visits   (B) used to visit
    (C) has visited   (D) have been visiting

( ) 4. Neil _____ on this topic for over thirty minutes, and I think
    he could go on for another half an hour.
    (A) lectures   (B) has been lecturing
    (C) used to lecture   (D) has to lecture

( ) 5. The case _____ to the police before we called 911.
    (A) reported   (B) was reporting
    (C) has reported   (D) had been reported

( ) 6. She _____ the restaurant when we arrive. We will not be able
    to see her in person.
    (A) has left (B) will have left (C) used to leave (D) is leaving

( ) 7. Tina had an _____ experience during the blind date.
    (A) embarrass   (B) embarrassment
    (C) embarrassed   (D) embarrassing

( ) 8. _____ the local custom, Kevin blundered again and again in
    the foreign country.
    (A) He no know   (B) Not knowing
    (C) He doesn't know   (D) Having not known

( ) 9. The interviewer talked to the guest with his hand _____ in the air.

(A) to wave   (B) waving

(C) waves   (D) waved

( ) 10. The pope _____ on the street, the crows pushed forward to see him in person.

(A) appeared   (B) appear

(C) are appearing   (D) appearing

( ) 11. Helen felt motivated with all her colleagues _____ her.

(A) to support   (B) supported

(C) supporting   (D) supportive

( ) 12. The program _____, the audience felt rather disappointed.

(A) suspend   (B) suspense

(C) to suspend   (D) being suspended

( ) 13. _____ fake news became more common, the government took some measures to stop the rumor from spreading.

(A) Compared with   (B) Regarding

(C) Providing   (D) Seeing that

( ) 14. _____ abroad, Kelly have been having video calls with her parents every day.

(A) While going   (B) After going

(C) To work   (D) She worked

( ) 15. The superstar walked down the Oscar red carpet, _____ to the reporters and fans.

(A) waved   (B) she waved

(C) waving   (D) having waved

Chapter 2
形容詞與關係詞

Part 1 | 形容詞變化概念：三級互通

1. 三級是可以互通的。

- He is the smartest boy in the class.
   - = He is smarter than anyone else in the class.
   - = He is smarter than any other boy in the class.
   - = No one else is as smart as he (is) in the class.
   他是班上最聰明的男孩。

2. 在使用比較的句型時，要注意到數目與人稱的一致。

❶ 同類型的事物才能比較。

❷ 兩所有物的比較，後者以所有格直接代替。

- His sneakers are much more expensive than mine.
   他的運動鞋比我的貴多了。

❸ 要比較的對象，單數或不可數名詞用that，複數名詞用those來替換前面提過的同概念名詞。

- The closet we saw in the furniture store was much bigger than that we have in our house.
   我們在傢俱店看到的衣櫥比我們家裡的大多了。

- According to the research, children attending school in the cities have more access to educational resources than those who are in the rural areas.
   根據研究，在城市裡上學的孩子比鄉下的孩子擁有更多的教育資源。

3. 比較級的用法中，若要強調「比……多得多」，可在比較級的形容詞或副詞前加上much、even、still、far及a lot等副詞來修飾。

4. 最高級可直接修飾名詞，形成S＋V＋最高級adj.＋N＋介詞片語的句型。

- Nothing is better than this. （比較級）

  = This is the best.（最高級）

  = This is as good as good can be.（對等比較）

  = What is better than this!（比較級）

  = Nothing is so good as this. （對等比較）

  沒有什麼比這個東西好（這個是最棒的）。

- The technology in Taiwan is as well-developed as that in the western countries.

  （→that代指the technology）

  台灣的科技和西方國家的一樣進步。

- The leaves of bread-fruit trees are wider than those of the pine trees.

  （→those代指the leaves）

  麵包樹的葉子比松樹的葉子來得大。

- She has as much patience as Florence Nightingale does.

  （→as...as 意指跟……一樣，兩動作的比較，後者以助動詞代替，does代指has much patience）

  她像南丁格爾一樣有耐心。

- Michael is the most diligent student in his class.

  （→最高級adj.＋N）

  麥可是他的班上最勤奮的學生。

- Play Station is one of the most popular game consoles in recent years.

  =Of all the game consoles in recent years, Play Station is one of the most popular.

  （→最高級adj.＋N）

  最近幾年的遊戲機裡，PS遊戲機是最受歡迎的。

( ) 1. Jerry is much _____ than his classmate.

  (A) friendly　　(B) friendliness　　(C) more friendly　　(D) friends

( ) 2. Linda is _____ than any other girl on her team.

  (A) the most ambitious　　　　(B) more ambitious

  (C) more ambition　　　　　　(D) less ambition

( ) 3. His report is nor as organized as _____ submitted by David.

  (A) that　　(B) which　　(C) the one which　　(D) those which

( ) 4. Nick has saved as much money as his brother _____.

  (A) does　　(B) has　　(C) saves　　(D) did

( ) 5.No one is _____ than Nina when dealing with the document. She is the most meticulous person in our company.

  (A) more careful　　　　(B) less careful

  (C) the most careless　　(D) the most careful

解答：(C) (B) (C) (D) (A)

Note

Part 2 | 關係代名詞的用法

 1. 關係代名詞及關係子句

1. 關係代名詞的種類

格 先行詞	主格	受格	所有格	子句內含介系詞時
人	who	whom	whose	by from whom of about
人以外的事物 （含動物）	which	which	whose (=...of which)	by in which on of
人、事物適用	that	that	that 所有格	That前 不加介系詞

關代的「格」小公式
1. 主格＋V
2. 受格＋S＋V
3. 受格＋S＋V＋prep.
4. prep.＋受格＋S＋V
5. 所有格＋N＋V

2. 關代的定義：連接詞＋代名詞

3. 先行詞定義：是被形容詞子句修飾的名詞，常在關代正前方

4. 關代的出現：缺什麼補什麼

- Last summer I went to Venice, which was called the City of Water.

  （→先行詞為**Venice**，關代為**which**作主詞，關係子句為**which is called the City of Water**）

  去年夏天我去了一趟威尼斯，那裡被稱為水都。

- A man who has discipline for himself can be good at people management.

  （→先行詞為**a man**，關代為**who**作主詞，關係子句為**who has discipline for himself**）

  一個有自我紀律的人，也許會擅長管理別人。

- David bought the designer coat which/that his girlfriend liked.

  （→先行詞為**the designer coat**，關代為**which/that**作受詞，關係子句為**which/that his girlfriend liked.**）

  大衛買了那件他女朋友喜歡的設計師外套。

- I noticed the cat whose paws are white.

  我注意到那隻腳掌是白色的貓。

延伸學習

1. 關代若為主格時，後面的**beV**或**V**的單複數由先行詞決定。

- The homeless cats which are healthy and energetic will be adopted by the kind woman.

  健康而且有精神的流浪貓將會被那個善心的女士收養。

2. 關代作為受格時，可被省略。

- There comes the woman whom/that we have met at the party last week.

  =There comes the woman we have met at the party last week.

  我們上週在派對上遇到的女士來了。

Test ━━ 快來即時測驗自己的學習成果吧！

( ) 1. God helps _____ help themselves.

    (A) those who   (B) that who (C) whose which   (D) that which

( ) 2. Jerry is the one _____ will take the position of the department manager.

    (A) who   (B) whom   (C) which   (D) that

( ) 3. The tangerines you gave me tasted better than _____ I bought at the market.

    (A) that   (B) which   (C) whom   (D) those which

( ) 4. Some _____ came to the office in an obtrusive manner asked to see our manager.

    (A) which   (B) whom   (C) who   (D) whose

( ) 5. Do you know that woman _____ son works at the local factory?

    (A) who   (B) whom   (C) whose   (D) whom

解答：(A) (A) (D) (C) (C)

Note

 **2. 修飾人的形容詞子句**

1. 句型結構

先行詞（人）	關代	動詞
he/she/it		
the person		
people	who	視先行詞決定單複數以及時態
those		
(any)one		

2. he/the (a) man/one who＋V... 表達同樣的意義，who引導的形容詞子句及主要子句的動詞用單數型。

3. 若who引導形容詞子句修飾先行詞為those/people/they時，形容詞子句及主要子句的動詞用複數型，用在先行詞為特別指稱特定人物時使用。

4. 此句型的關係代名詞，固定用who，不用that。

5. 此句型除了放在主要子句的主詞位置外，也可以放在受詞位置。

- **God helps those who help themselves.**
  （→先行詞為受詞those，關代動為複數型）天助自助者。

- **Those who are more meticulous are more likely to succeed.**
  （→先行詞為主詞those，主句動詞及關代動詞為複數型）
  謹慎的人比較可能成功。

- **One who intrudes others' privacy will be punished.**
  = Those who intrude others' privacy will be punished.
  （→先行詞為主詞one，主句動詞及關代動詞為單數型；先行詞為主詞those，主句動詞及關代動詞為複數型）
  侵犯他人隱私的人會受罰。

- He who is content is happy. => Happy is he who is content.

（→第一句的關係子句在主詞，第二句在受詞）

知足者常樂。

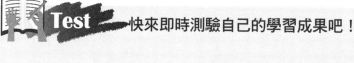

快來即時測驗自己的學習成果吧！

( ) 1. He _____ follows the principles will be treated with courtesy.

(A) who   (B) which   (C) that   (D) those

( ) 2. Those _____ help others would feel content.

(A) that   (B) whom   (C) which   (D) who

( ) 3. People _____ spread rumors on the Internet would be punished.

(A) that   (B) who   (C) which   (D) whom

( ) 4. _____ blesses others is abundantly blessed.

(A) Those who   B) The one who

(C) The one that   (D) Those that

( ) 5._____ plan to change their contact phone numbers should inform the HR office.

(A) Those who   (B) Those that

(C) He who   (D) That who

解答：(A) (D) (B) (B) (A)

 **3. 介系詞＋which**

1. 句型結構

先行詞（人）	介系詞＋關代	關係子句
事／物	in by　which with	完整子句
人	to by　whom with	完整子句

2. 此句型中，**which**為關係代名詞，做介系詞in/by/with……等的受詞。

3. 此句型中，**which**因為前面有介系詞，所以不可以替換為that。

4. 此句型中，「介系詞＋which」之後須接完整的形容詞子句（子句中不缺主詞或受詞）。

5. 此句型中，介系詞也可以放在關係子句的最後面。

6. 此句型中，**which**若替換成**whom**也有類似的用法，但先行詞必須為「人」。

- My father gave me a smartphone with which I can look up information on the Internet wherever I go.
  （→先行詞為物laptop，介系詞with，關代which）
  我父親送給我一部無論我到哪裡都可以上網查詢資訊的智慧型手機。

- The police urged that people keep away from the hospital in which the patients of pneumonia are taken under quarantine.
  = The police urged that people keep away from the hospital which the patients of pneumonia are taken under quarantine in. （→先行詞為物hospital，介系詞in，關代which，介系詞可置於關係子句的最後面）
  警方力勸民眾遠離肺炎病患被隔離的醫院。

- Looking back, we may see the bus station from which we departed.

= Looking back, we may see the bus station which we departed from.（→先行詞為物bus station，介系詞from，關代which，介系詞可置於關係子句的最後面）
往回看，我們可以看到我們出發的公車站。

• Gary is the person from whom everyone would ask for advice.
（→先行詞為人the person，介系詞from，關代whom）
蓋瑞是大家都喜歡向他尋求建議的人。

延伸學習

in that（因為）是連接詞，後面接表原因的子句。

• To tell the truth, I don't like her in that she is a girl who enjoying being flattered.
説實話，我不喜歡她，因為她是喜歡被恭維的女孩子。

Test ——快來即時測驗自己的學習成果吧！

( ) 1. Helen is a person _____ everyone in her office like to talk.
(A) whom　　(B) who　　　　(C) with whom　(D) to that

( ) 2. That is the house _____ my grandparents used to live five years ago.
(A) by whom　(B) in which　　(C) with who　(D) for which

( ) 3. Laurie is the person _____ the book was edited.
(A) by whom　(B) with whom　(C) in that　　(D) from which

( ) 4. Emma is the girl _____ the love letter should have been sent.
(A) from whom　(B) to whom　　(C) with which　(D) by which

( ) 5.This is the gadget _____ you can cook meat and vegetables easily.
(A) to which　(B) from whom　(C) by which　(D) with which

解答：(C) (B) (A) (B) (D)

 **4. 數量形容詞片語＋關代**

1. 句型結構

先行詞	數量形容詞片語＋關代	關係子句
人	which	
	some of	以which或whom為主詞的補述句
物	whom	

2. 此句型中，**whom/which**為關係代名詞，引導一補述用法的形容詞子句，**whom/which**做子句中的主詞。

3. 此句型中，**whom/which**也是連接詞，連接前後兩個句子，**whom**代替前面句子提過的人，**which**代替前面句子提過事或物。

4. 表示數量的片語如：some of, many of, most of, none of, two of, half of, both of, neither of, each of, all of, several of, a few of, little of, a number of置於代名詞之前，只能使用whom或it。

5. 此句型中，**whom/which**除了是兩個句子的連接詞外，也是為其引導的形容詞子句之受詞。

6. 以數量形容詞片語引導的形容詞子句之前要加逗號。

- With the prevalence of cell phones, lots of cellular base stations are built up in the mountain areas, and some endangered animals may live in those areas. .

  = With the prevalence of cell phones, lots of cellular base stations are built up in the mountain areas, some of which the endangered animals may live in.

  （→which為連接詞，也是受詞these areas）

  隨著手機的普及，許多電信基地台蓋在山區，其中有些地方可能是瀕危動物的棲息地。

- Many fans follow these Internet celebrities, and the advertisers may ask some of those Internet celebrities to promote special products.

= Many fans follow these Internet celebrities, some of whom may be asked to promote products by some advertisers.

（→whom為連接詞，也是受詞those celebrities）

許多粉絲會追蹤這些網紅，而廣告商會找其中一些網紅代言某些產品。

Test ━━快來即時測驗自己的學習成果吧！

( ) 1. These are the songs composed by Jay Chou, _____ have been rendered by famous singers.

(A) some of which (B) those who (C) that which (D) some of whom

( ) 2. Helen bought many apples at the market, _____ were still green.

(A) some of whom   (B) some of which

(C) one of which   (D) one of whom

( ) 3. Many protesters gathered in front of the city government, _____ wore the scarfs with a pattern of the national flag.

(A) with which   (B) by whom

(C) some of whom   (D) some of which

( ) 4. The subculture in the school has great influence on the students, _____ are panicked about not being different from their peers.

(A) those who   (B) those which

(C) some of those   (D) some of whom

( ) 5. The TV series has been fascinating to youngsters, _____ even dress themselves up as the characters in the story.

(A) some of whom   (B) those who

(C) some of which   (D) many of which

解答：(A) (B) (C) (D) (A)

Part 3 | 含先行詞的關代：what

 複合關係代名詞what

1. 定義：what本身是先行詞，也是關係代名詞，引導名詞子句，故what之前不可再有先行詞。

2. what引導的子句為名詞子句，做主要句的主詞、受詞或補語，作主詞時，其後動詞用單數。

- The company is different from what it was/used to be ten years ago.

（→先行詞和關代應為the company which，由what取代，作主詞）

這間公司和十年前大不相同。

- No one can predict what she would say next.

（→先行詞和關代應為the thing which，由what取代，作受詞）

沒人能預測接下來她會說什麼。

- What I am concerned about is the company's financial condition.（→先行詞和關代應為the thing which，由what取代，作受詞）我所擔心的是這間公司的財務狀況。

- Answer what you think is relevant.

（→先行詞和關代應為anything that，由what取代，作主詞）

回答你認為相關的事。

注意要點

此句型也常合併起來在同一個句子中做比較。

- We should not judge a man by what he has but by what he is.
  我們不應該以一個人的財富來判斷這個人，而是要以他的為人來判斷。（what one is：一個人的為人；what one has：一個人的財富）

what有關的慣用語與句型

1. what is better →更好的是

2. what is worse→更糟的是

3. what we call/what is called = (the) so-called = and that is →所謂的

4. what I am today →今天的我

5. A is to B what C is to D →A之於B猶如C之於D

6. what with A and (what with) B →半因……半因……

7. what by A and what by B →半藉……半藉……

- The consultant is enthusiastic; what's more, his advice are very useful. 這位顧問很熱心；此外，他的建議很有用。

- What with lateness and what with his bad manner, he left a poor impression on the interviewers.
  一半因為遲到，一半因為態度不佳，所以他給面試官留下了不好的印象。

 ……必須要做的事就是……

1. 句型架構

All (that)
What   + S + [have (has) / had] to do [is / was] + (to) + V …
The only thing

2. 此句型中的**what**為複合關係代名詞，引導名詞子句作主要子句的主詞，用單數動詞（**is/was**），不定詞（**to V**）作主詞補語。

3. 動詞**is/was**之後也可以接原型動詞（**VR**）。

4. what可用**all that**來替換，**that**為關代可省略。

- In my opinion, what everyone has to do to prevent an outbreak of an epidemic is to have good personal hygiene.
  依我之見，每個人為了預防疫情爆發應該要做的事情就是保持個人衛生。

- To improve your English speaking proficiency, all you have to do is to practice every day.
  為了增進英語口說能力，你所需要做的就是每天練習。

have/has/had to的意思是「必須」，視句子意義可用其他動詞片語替換。

- **What I can do is give Max a hug to make him feel better.**

  我所能做的就是給麥克斯一個擁抱讓他覺得好過些。

- **All you need to do is restart the computer, and the system will be normal again.**

  你所需要做的就是重新啟動電腦，系統就會恢復正常了。

Test 快來即時測驗自己的學習成果吧！

( ) 1. The gadget can improve your work proficiency. _____, it is affordable for most salary workers.

  (A) What we call   (B) What is better

  (C) What is worse   (D) What I can do

( ) 2. _____ we could do for her is to complete the form.

  (A) Everything which   (B) All those   (C) What   (D) Whatever

( ) 3. To have the event go smoothly, _____ you can do is to check everything in the event rehearsal.

  (A) the things   (B) that   (C) those which   (D) what

( ) 4. _____ she could do for her son was to offer him guidance during times of trouble.

  (A) All   (B) The thing what   (C) That which   (D) Everything which

( ) 5. The teachers have said _____ he wanted to tell his students.

  (A) what that   (B) all that   (C) the things   (D) all needed

解答：(B) (C) (D) (A) (B)

Part 4 | 關係副詞及關係子句

 1. 關係副詞

1. 關係副詞的定義

❶ 關係副詞為連接詞＋副詞=連接詞＋介系詞＋名詞（代名詞）
=介系詞＋關係代名詞

❷ 關係副詞連接完整子句就會是名詞子句

2. 關係副詞的種類

先行詞 ╲ 功能	副詞兼連接詞	（相等語）介詞＋關代
地點（place）	where	in/on which at/from
時間（time）	when	in/on which at/during
理由（reason）	why	= (for) which
方式（way, manner）	how	= (in) which

3. 關係副詞的範例

介系詞＋先行詞	先行詞	介系詞＋關代＋關係子句
at the speed	the speed	(at which) ＋S＋V
at the rate	the rate	(at which) ＋S＋V

by the method	the method	(by which) ＋S＋V
by the process	the process	(by which) ＋S＋V
to the extent	the extent	(to which) ＋S＋V
against the standard	the standard	(against which) ＋S＋V
in the 1990's	the 1990's	(in which) ＋S＋V
during the 1990's	the 1990's	(during which) ＋S＋V
in Taipei	Taipei	(in which) ＋S＋V

- 原句：**This is the company and I work in the company.**

  → **This is the company and in the company I work.**

  （→連接詞＋介詞＋名詞）

  → **This is the company in which I work.**（→介詞＋關代）

  → **This is the company where I work.**（→關副）

  我在這間公司工作。

- 原句：**Entertaining clients is the way and he got the deal by entertaining clients.**

  → **Entertaining clients is the way and by entertaining clients he got the deal.**（→連接詞＋介詞＋名詞）

  → **Entertaining clients is the way by which he got the deal.**

  （→介詞＋關代）

  → **Entertaining clients is the way how he got the deal.**（→關副）

  和客戶應酬就是他獲得這筆交易的方式。

- **This is the reason and for the reason he got hired.**

  （→連接詞＋介詞＋名詞）

  → **This is the reason for which he got hired.**（→介詞＋關代）

  → **This is the reason why he got hired.**（→關副）

  這是他為什麼被雇用的原因。

- The Age of Enlightenment is the period in which philosophers proposed famous theories.（→介詞＋關代）

  = The Age of Enlightenment is the period when philosophers proposed famous theories.（→關副）

  啟蒙時期就是哲學家提出著名理論的時期。

- Anyone whose house is damaged in the wildfire can get subsidies from the government.

  （→根據句意，應用表所有格的whose表示house屬於anyone。）
  任何人房屋因為野火受到損害都可以獲得政府補助。

- The workers are repairing the apartment whose pipes are leaking.

  （→根據句意，應用所有格的 whose或是of which來表示pipes屬於the apartment。）
  那些工人在整修的那間公寓，水管在漏水。

- The troll on the Internet for whose sake she is suffering this hardship remains anonymous.

  （→for one's sake「為了某人的緣故」，形容詞子句中應用whose來取代one's。）

  造成她受到這些苦難的網路酸民身份仍然不明。

 2. 表達「這就是為何……」的句型

1. 說明

❶ 這是簡化的「解釋」句型，使句子更簡潔。句型為：That's why/how/...＋S＋V... 那就是為何／如何的……（原因／方法）

❷ 關係副詞why/how/when/where語意上省略前面的先行詞the reason/the way/the time/the place，後面則接名詞子句。

❸ 此句型也常保留先行詞而省略關係副詞，也就是That's the reason/the way...。惟需注意the way與how不可連用。

- She exercises at least thirty minutes a day. That's how/the way that/the way in which she can keep in shape.
  她每天運動至少三十分鐘。那就是她能維持好身材的方法。

- He always teases his classmates. That's (the reason) why <u>he is never well received by his peers.</u>

  他總是嘲笑他的同學。那就是為什麼他在同儕之間不受歡迎的原因。

- That's how the newly-opened museum attracts visitors. (○)

  That's the way how the newly-opened museum attracts visitors. (✗)

  那就是這家新開的博物館吸引參觀者的方法。

Test ——快來即時測驗自己的學習成果吧！

( ) 1. That is the restaurant _____ my parents first met each other many years ago.

(A) which   (B) where   (C) when   (D) why

( ) 2. She didn't explain _____ she was absent from the meeting.

(A) when   (B) which

(C) the reason which   (D) why

( ) 3. Laurie is hanging a sign on the tree _____ branches climb over the tree.

(A) which   (B) that   (C) how   (D) whose

( ) 4. Keeping a balanced diet is _____ the man remains healthy.

(A) of which   (B) in that

(C) the way by which   (D) when

( ) 5. The critique _____ comment on the latest film went viral on the Internet was found holding a fake diploma.

(A) whose   (B) that   (C) how   (D) when

解答：(B) (D) (D) (C) (A)

Part 5 | 複合關係副詞

1. 定義：

　　複合關係副詞，顧名思義就是在原有的關係詞上加上ever。使文意增加了「無論」或「任何」。

2. 引導副詞子句時，複合關係副詞對等列表

whatever = no matter what. 無論什麼

whoever = no matter who(m) 無論是誰

whichever = no matter which 無論哪一個

whenever = no matter when 無論何時

wherever = no matter where 無論何處

however = no matter how 無論如何

- Whichever company wins the bidding, it will make no difference to me. 無論哪個公司得標，對我來說都是一樣的。
- However difficult the problem is, you should not give up easily.
  無論問題有多困難，你都不應該輕易放棄。
- You may call the consultant whenever you have any work-related questions. 你可以在任何遇到工作相關問題時打電話給顧問。
- You can choose the red carpet or the gray carpet. Whichever is one thousand hundred dollars.
  （→whichever 用做主詞）
  你可以選擇紅色或灰色的地毯。價錢都是一千元。
- The officer is determined to reject whatever he regards as bribery. （→用whatever接後面缺受詞的子句。）
  官員決心要拒絕任何他認為是賄賂的東西。

- I admire the creativity of the designer, so I like all his works, for whatever reason.（→用whatever修飾後面的名詞。）

  我欣賞這位設計師的創意,所以我喜歡他的所有作品,無論是出於什麼理由。

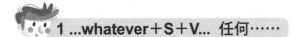

1 ...whatever＋S＋V... 任何……

1. whatever為複合關係代名詞,等於anything that,引導名詞子句,指事或物,但不能指人,為what的強調用法。

2. 此句型中,主要子句為不完整子句(即子句缺主詞、受詞或補語),而whatever引導的名詞子句可作為主要子句的主詞、受詞或補語。

- Whatever she says is considered precious teaching for me.
  （→whatever she says 為整句主詞）

  她所說的任何話,我都當作是金玉良言。

- When the exam was over, he could do whatever he wanted.
  （→whatever he liked為整句受詞）

  當考試結束後,他就可以做任何想做的事情。

- The best remedy for her is whatever helps her get rid of the traumatic memory.
  （→whatever he liked為整句補語）

  對她最好的療法就是任何可以幫助她擺脫創傷經驗的事物。

延伸學習

whatever後面若引導副詞子句,則意義為「無論什麼……」,相當於「no matter what...」。

- Whatever the outcome may be, he has done his best in this competition.

  = No matter what the outcome may be, he has done his best in this competition.

  無論結果是什麼,他已經在比賽中盡力了。

- Whatever the religious leader does would be appreciated by his followers. （→名詞子句）

  這位宗教領袖做的任何事情都會被他的追隨者崇拜。

- Whatever you purchase at the store, you should keep the receipt for at least seven days. （→副詞子句）

  無論你在這家店買什麼，你都應該保存收據七天。

- Whatever is publicized on mass media has a great influence on the viewers. （→名詞子句）

  在大眾媒體上公開的任何事情對觀眾都有很大的影響。

- Remember not to trust whatever the con artist tells you. （→名詞子句）

  記得別相信這個詐騙高手告訴你的任何事。

Test ——快來即時測驗自己的學習成果吧！

( ) 1. _____ the controversial（爭議的）person posted on the social network website was regarded dubious（可疑的）.

(A) No matter when (B) What (C) Which (D) Whatever

( ) 2. The politician denied _____ was reported in the tabloid newspaper.

(A) whichever (B) whenever (C) whatever (D) whoever

( ) 3. _____ they did for the project was considered confidential.

(A) That (B) Whatever (C) The things which (D) Whoever

( ) 4. I appreciated _____ she did to reach a robust conclusion for the research.

(A) whichever (B) no matter how (C) wherever (D) whatever

( ) 5. Jerry would do _____ he could to help the refugees.

(A) whatever (B) whichever (C) however (D) whenever

解答：(D) (C) (B) (D) (A)

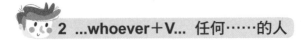

2 ...whoever＋V... 任何……的人

1. 此句型中，whoever為複合關係代名詞，等於anyone who、he who、one who、the (a) man who，是主格用法，後面接單數動詞。

2. 複合關係代名詞是當主格或受格，與前面的介系詞或動詞無關，而是以其在所引導的名詞子句的地位而定。

3. whoever為後面引導的名詞子句的主詞，同時此名詞子句也是主要的主詞。

4. whoever本身為後面引導的名詞子句的主詞，但其所引導的名詞子句則為主要句的受詞，不因介系詞with之故而用whomever。

● Whoever wants to enter the venue should show his ID card.
（→whoever為名詞子句的主詞，整個名詞子句為句子的主詞）
凡想進入活動場地的人需要出示身份證明。

● Whoever has questions about the latest policy can refer to the announcement on the official website of the local government.
（→whoever為名詞子句的主詞，整個名詞子句為主句的主詞）
任何對最新政策有疑問的人都可以參考地方政府的官方網站上的最新公告。

● Please send this notice to whoever intends to participate in the program.
（→whoever為名詞子句的主詞，整個名詞子句為主句的主詞）
請將這則通知傳給任何想參加這個計畫的人。

延伸學習

whoever除了當複合關係代名詞外，也可以當複合關係副詞，相當於no matter who，後面引導副詞子句，解釋為「不論誰」。

以下例句中，whoever引導表讓步的副詞子句，whoever為子句中的主詞，同時也是整個句子的連接詞。

- Whoever is hosting the event, it would be very popular among teenagers.

  = No matter who is hosting the event, it would be very popular among the teenagers.

  無論是誰主辦這個活動，它都會很受青少年歡迎。

- Whoever finds the lost document, please send it to the police station in the community.

  = No matter who finds the lost document, please send it to the police station in the community.

  無論是誰找到遺失的文件，請將它送到社區的警察局。

Test —— 快來即時測驗自己的學習成果吧！

( ) 1. Please reveal this information to _____ is interests in computer programming.

(A) whatever   (B) whichever   (C) whoever   (D) wherever

( ) 2. _____ has financial difficulty can apply for the subsidy.

(A) However   (B) Whoever   (C) Whichever   (D) Whatever

( ) 3. _____ uses the laboratory should register in the company's system.

(A) Whatever   (B) Whichever   (C) Whoever   (D) Whenever

( ) 4. _____ notices a mistake in the play script, please inform its writer.

(A) Those   (B) Someone   (C) The person   (D) Whoever

( ) 5. The generous lady would assist _____ is in need of financial aid.

(A) whoever   (B) someone   (C) the people   (D) anyone

解答：(C) (B) (C) (D) (A)

3. whenever＋S＋V 無論何時、每次……

wherever＋S＋V 無論何處...

however＋adj./adv.＋S＋V 無論如何

　　whenever為複合關係代名詞，等於every time以及no matter when，引導表時間的副詞子句。

　　wherever則等於no matter where引導表地方的副詞子句。however後面則一定要接 adj./adv.，表示無論……的狀態。

- Every time she was in a good mood, she bought light refreshments for her colleagues.

  = Whenever she was in a good mood, she bought light refreshments for her colleagues.

  = No matter when she was in a good mood, she bought light refreshments for her colleagues.

  每次她心情好時，她就會買茶點給她同事。

- Wherever Gina traveled, she would taste the local delicacies.

  = No matter where Gina traveled, she would taste the local delicacies.

  不管吉娜旅行到何處，她都會去品嚐當地的美食。

- However challenging the project is, she is determined to accomplish it.

  = No matter how challenging the project is, she is determined to accomplish it.

  無論這個計畫多具有挑戰性，她都決心要完成它。

- However cautiously you plan for the rundown of the event, there would still be glitches in the process.

  = No matter how cautiously you plan for the rundown of the event, there would still be glitches in the process.

  不管你多謹慎地規劃活動流程，還是有可能出現小問題。

Test —快來即時測驗自己的學習成果吧！

( ) 1. You can refer to the online encyclopedia _____ you have questions while doing your report.

(A) whatever　(B) whichever　(C) whenever　(D) wherever

( ) 2. _____ hard she tried to please her parents, they gave her the cold shoulder.

(A) However　(B) Whoever　(C) Whichever　(D) Whatever

( ) 3. Helen carries her old backpack _____ she goes.

(A) whatever　(B) wherever　(C) whoever　(D) whenever

( ) 4. She promised that she would be there for me _____ I need help.

(A) whoever　(B) wherever　(C) whenever　(D) whatever

( ) 5. They would reach the peak of the mountain _____ difficult it may seem.

(A) how　　　　　　　　　(B) no matter how

(C) though　　　　　　　　(D) as

解答：(C) (A) (B) (C) (B)

Note

_____

_____

_____

_____

_____

_____

Part **6** | 關係代名詞 that的限定用法

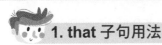 **1. that 子句用法**

在以下情況時，所有的關係代名詞都只能用that表示。

❶ 最高級形容詞，如：the greatest/the smallest

❷ 序數，如：the first/the last

❸ 限定意義較強的形容詞，如：the only/the main/the chief/the very

❹ 先行詞為：no/any/all/both/much/each/every/anything

❺ 先行詞為：人與非人並列時

❻ 先行詞為：who/which為首的問句為避免重覆

❼ that 之前無逗點及介系詞

• **This is the very store that John talked about the other day.**
（→先行詞限定意義強）

這就是約翰上次提到的那家店。

• **He is one of the most well-mannered person that I have ever met.**（→先行詞為最高級形容詞）

他是我遇到過最彬彬有禮的人之一。

• **Was it you or the wind that shut the window?**
（→先行詞為人與非人並列）

是你還是風把窗戶關上的？

• **Boughs that bear most hang lowest.**（→諺語用法）
肚大能容。

 2. 分裂強調句It is/was＋強調部分＋ that（關代）＋剩餘結構

sb → who / whom
sth. → which
地方副詞 → where
時間副詞 → when

• James planted camellias in the garden two years ago.
詹姆士兩年前在花園種植了山茶花。

→It was James <u>that planted camellias</u> in the garden two years ago. 兩年前在花園種植山茶花的是詹姆士。

→It was camellias <u>that James planted</u> in garden two years ago. 詹姆士兩年前在花園種植的是山茶花。

→It was in the garden <u>that James planted camellias</u> two years ago. 詹姆士兩年前種植山茶花的地方是花園。

→It was two years ago <u>that James planted camellias</u> in garden. 詹姆士在花園種植山茶花是兩年前的事。

Test ——快來即時測驗自己的學習成果吧！

( ) 1. This is the only TV program _____ I would allow my kid to watch.
(A) which　　(B) that　　(C) whom　　(D) whose

( ) 2. She is one of the most diligent students _____ I have met in recent years.
(A) who　　(B) which　　(C) whom　　(D) that

( ) 3. It was the year 2000 _____ the first election of president and vice president in Taiwan was held.
(A) the year that　(B) when　　(C) from which　(D) since then

( ) 4. It was Jerry _____ took care of the dogs in the animal shelter.
(A) by whom　(B) that　　(C) whose　　(D) which

( ) 5. It was last year _____ the company organized the employee welfare committee.
(A) which　　(B) where　　(C) who　　(D) that

解答：(B) (D) (B) (B) (D)

Part 7 | 關係子句的限定及非限定用法

	限定用法	非限定用法
定義	修飾並限定先行詞	補充、說明、唯一或專指之先行詞
形式	關代之前沒逗點	關代之前有逗點
特性	1. 可使用關代that 2. 關代為受格時可省略	1. 不可使用關代that 2. 關代為受格不可省

- **I met Jerry's girlfriend who takes a part-time job at the McDonald's.**

  （→Jerry's girlfriend ≧2）

  我遇到Jerry在麥當勞打工的女朋友。

- **I met Jerry's girlfriend, who takes a part-time job at the McDonald's.**

  （→Jerry's girlfriend=1）

  我遇到Jerry的女朋友，她在麥當勞打工。

- **The clerk, whom many customers have complained about, just resigned from her job.**

  （→The clerk =1）

  那個許多顧客抱怨過的櫃檯人員，剛剛辭職。

  > 關代之前有逗點 →非限定用法 →後翻譯
  >
  > 關代之前無逗點 →限定用法 →先翻譯

- **She lives in a mansion (X) which is located in the outskirts of the city.** 她住在城市近郊的別墅裡。

- Vivian, who speaks Spanish, applied for the international job vacancy.
  會說西班牙文的薇薇安，申請國際的工作職缺。

- Coffee (,) which is grown much of the world, is considered a cash crop.
  在許多國家都有種植的咖啡，被認為是一種經濟作物。

Test ─快來即時測驗自己的學習成果吧！

( ) 1. Professor Chang _____ is required for the program, tends to give high scores to his students.

    (A) , who   (B) who   (C) , that   (D) that

( ) 2. Peter spends most of his time studying math _____ is his favorite subject.

    (A) , who   (B) who   (C) , which   (D) which

( ) 3. I visited the gallery _____ was opened last month.

    (A) , which   (B) which   (C) where   (D) when

( ) 4. I met Mandy's cousin _____ is studying in the medical school.

    (A) whom   (B) who   (C) whose   (D) which

( ) 5. Fiona _____ is considering changing her major, would consult her mentor.

    (A) which   (B) where   (C) , who   (D) , that

解答：(C) (A) (C) (B) (B) (C)

Chapter2 形容詞與關係詞

Part 8 | 準關代 as/but/than

 1. as為準關係代名詞

as 原為從屬連接詞引導副詞子句,但與下列三種情形連用時,因其代名詞功能造成子句之不完整卻又具有連接詞功能稱之為「準關代」。

1. as...as

- We will do as much as we can.
  我們會盡力而為。

- You can take as many as you want.
  你可以盡量拿。

2. such...as

- Don't make such friends as will downgrade your morals.
  不要結交會使你道德降低的朋友。

- Don't share such information as you haven't verified.
  不要傳播你尚未求證的資訊。

3. the same...as

- I have the same opinions as you have.
  我有跟你一樣的意見。

- I want to buy the same purse as you have.
  我要買和你一樣的皮包。

- This is the brand that/which the actress is promoting.

  = This is the brand that/which the actress is promoting.

  = This is the same brand as the actress is promoting.

  = This is the same brand as is being promoted by the actress.
  這就是那位女星正在代言的品牌。

 **2. but為準關係代名詞**

1. 此句型中，**but**為準關係代名詞，引導形容詞子句，可做主詞或受詞。

2. but本身的意義是否定的，相當於「**...that...not...**」，或者是「**without＋V-ing**」，否定字**no**相當於「**not a**」。

3. but之前否定詞，形成雙重否定的句子，表達肯定的意思。

• This gourmet often boasts that there is no cuisine but he has tasted.

= This gourmet often boasts that there is not a cuisine that he has not tasted.

= This gourmet often boasts that he has tasted all cuisines.

這個美食家常吹噓說沒有他沒品嚐過的菜餚。

• My mother often told me that there was no difficulty but could be overcome in the world.

我媽媽常告訴我世界上沒有克服不了的難關。

4. but之前的否定詞，除了**no**之外，常用的還有**never**、**seldom**、**hardly**、**scarcely**、**not**、**few**、**little**等。

• We know scarcely any teenagers but indulge themselves in spending time on smartphones.

我們認識的當中鮮少有不沉迷使用手機的。

5.「**...not/never...without＋V-ing**」亦可表達肯定意義的句型，意為「沒有……不……」或「每……必……」。

• Gary never travels overseas without bringing back a lot of souvenirs.

蓋瑞每次出國旅行一定會帶很多紀念品回國。

3. than 作為準關係代名詞

1. than為準關係代名詞，引導形容詞子句，修飾帶有比較級的先行詞。

2. 此形容詞子句須為缺受詞或主詞的不完整子句。

- The project has helped more poor children than was expected.
  這項計劃幫助的貧童比預期更多。

- It is inappropriate to use more medical resource than you need.
  使用比你需要的還多醫療資源是不適當的。

- Come to the conference. Maybe you'll meet more scholars than you expected.
  來參加研討會吧！也許你會遇到比預期更多的學者。

- Geologist gained more useful data than had been expected.
  地質學家得到比預期更多的資料。

Note

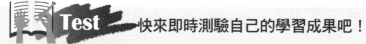

( ) 1. Kevin shared as much _____ he knew about the theme with the students.

    (A) as   (B) what   (C) which   (D) than

( ) 2. It is said the number of refugees is much higher _____ publicized by the government.

    (A) as   (B) than   (C) but   (D) such

( ) 3. We should never expose ourselves to such substances _____ would damage our health.

    (A) that   (B) which   (C) as   (D) than

( ) 4. The tailor claims that there is no type of outfit _____ he could not make.

    (A) as   (B) such   (C) than   (D) but

( ) 5. The musical did not attracted _____ viewers as predicted.

    (A) as much as   (B) more than

    (C) as many as   (D) the same as

解答：(A) (B) (C) (D) (C)

( ) 1. The city is full of things _____ the kids would feel excited.
 (A) that   (B) which   (C) in that   (D) about which

( ) 2. The test candidate _____ forgot to bring his ID was not allowed into the examination room.
 (A) who   (B) , who   (C) which   (D) whom

( ) 3. The person _____ the package was sent has moved away.
 (A) whom   (B) who   (C) to whom   (D) for which

( ) 4. Fiona didn't specify _____ she would reject the job offer in her email.
 (A) the reason   (B) why   (C) for which   (D) the way which

( ) 5. The paparazzi for _____ sake Princess Diana got killed in a car accident was blamed by the public.
 (A) who   (B) whom   (C) whose   (D) which

( ) 6. She would forward no article _____ by the authorities.
 (A) but is verified   (B) as verifies   (C) but verifies   (D) for verifying

( ) 7. _____ is known to all, washing hands before meals is a good habit.
 (A) What   (B) That   (C) Such   (D) As

( ) 8. It was in 2004 _____ Taipei 101 was officially opened.
 (A) which   (B) that   (C) how   (D) what

( ) 9. You can report your problem to _____ is available at our customer service department.
 (A) whoever   (B) whatever   (C) however   (D) whenever

( ) 10. The clerk asked me to indicate _____ the package contained on the label.

(A) who   (B) that   (C) which   (D) what

( ) 11. Being patient and friendly is _____ he won the clients' trust.

(A) the reason which   (B) the way in which
(C) with which   (D) by which

( ) 12. Mr. Spenser _____ reviewed your manuscript, has sent you his comments.

(A) who   (B) , who   (C) by whom   (D) that

( ) 13. Your jacket looks fashionable. I want to buy _____ yours.

(A) the same jacket as   (B) such one like
(C) as good as the one   (D) the same as

( ) 14. Sarah is one of the most creative writers _____ I have known.

(A) who   (B) whom   (C) that   (D) which

( ) 15. This is the museum _____ I volunteered as a docent five years ago.

(A) when   (B) where   (C) that   (D) which

Chapter 3
形容詞與關係詞

Part 1 | 名詞子句

 **1. 名詞子句的意義**

名詞子句的文法意義等同於名詞,與名詞片語相同,都具有:主詞、受詞、補語、同位語的功能。其結構皆為連接詞+完整句子,可置於句首、句中或句尾。名詞子句→當名詞用,包括:

❶ that子句

❷ 表是否(whether/if)的名詞子句

❸ 複合關代的名詞子句

❹ 意志動詞的名詞子句

❺ 疑問詞引導的間接問句

名詞子句的功能包括:

1. 作為主詞:

• <u>That the sun rises in the east</u> is true.
太陽從東邊升起是個事實。

• <u>That smoking does damage to people's health</u> is a fact.
吸菸對人們的健康有害是個事實。

2. 作為受詞:

• I hope <u>that Gina will come back safe and sound.</u>
我希望吉娜會平安回來。

• This story teaches us <u>that we should be generous to others.</u>
這個故事告訴我們應該對人慷慨。

• My parents have made <u>what I am today.</u>
我的父母成就了今日的我。

3. 作為補語：

● She is not <u>what she used to be.</u>
她已經不是從前的她了。

● The reason why he was late for the meeting is <u>that he went to a wrong meeting room.</u>
他開會遲到的原因是他走錯會議室了。

4. 作為同位語：

● The theory <u>that electronic cigarette causes cancer</u> is not proved yet.
電子菸誘發癌症的理論還沒有被證實。

● His attitude shows <u>that he is indecisive on this matter.</u>
他的態度顯示他對這件事猶豫不決。

Test 快來即時測驗自己的學習成果吧！

( ) 1. _____ the Earth is round is a fact.

    (A) That   (B) What   (C) This   (D) Which

( ) 2. Wendy wondered _____ the door of the laboratory was locked or not.

    (A) if   (B) that   (C) whether   (D) why

( ) 3. This is different from _____ she told me.

    (A) what   (B) which   (C) that   (D) which

( ) 4. Kevin knew_____ her daughter didn't mean to offend him.

    (A) what   (B) whether   (C) if   (D) that

( ) 5. The sign indicates _____ the road ahead is under repair.

    (A) that   (B) whether   (C) which   (D) if

解答：(A) (C) (A) (D) (A)

3

子句與五大句型

2. that/whether/if 引導之名詞子句

1. 以that為引導的名詞子句

一般以that＋子句=名詞子句的形式最常見，通常可省略，但置於句首時則不行。而that引導的名詞子句做「主詞」時，可換為 "It is＋adj.＋that＋S＋V"

- **It is wonderful <u>that we will have a long vacation</u>.**
  我們將可以放長假，這真是太棒了。

- **My mentor told me <u>that I shouldn't be frustrated about this failure.</u>** （→名詞子句做受詞）
  我的導師告訴我，不應該為了這次挫折感到氣餒。

- **Another good reason for using video conferencing system is <u>that people can save the time spent on transportation</u>.**
  （→名詞子句做補語）
  另一個使用視訊會議系統的好理由是人們可以節省交通運輸的時間。

- **<u>That we will have a longer vacation</u> is wonderful.**
  （→名詞子句做主詞）
  我們可以有更長的假期，這真是太棒了。

- **Mary told me the good news <u>that she won a prize in the designer competition</u>.** （→名詞子句做同位語）
  瑪莉告訴我一個好消息：她在設計比賽中得獎了。

2. 以whether/ if（是否⋯⋯）引導的名詞子句

whether和if都可當做「是否」解釋，並引導名詞子句做受詞。但「if＋子句」做受詞時，後面不可接 or not。

- **I don't know whether <u>he will show up or not</u>.**
  （→名詞子句做受詞）= I don't know if <u>he will show up</u>.
  我不知道他是否會出現。

- **Tell me whether Brian will take the position<u> or not</u>.**
  （→名詞子句做受詞）= Tell me if <u>Brian will take the position</u>.
  告訴我布萊恩會不會接受這個職務。

- I want to know whether/if <u>the endangered animals survived natural disaster.</u>

（→名詞子句做受詞）。

我想知道遭遇危險的動物是否有在這次天災中存活下來。

whether 引導的名詞子句可當主詞，但if則不可。

- Whether the company will make profit remains unknown. (O)

  If the company will make profit remains unknown. (X)

  公司會不會賺錢仍然是未知的。

3. What與複合關代，通常用來引導做主詞或受詞的名詞子句

- What she did was wrong.

（→名詞子句做主詞）

她所做的事情是錯誤的。

- The host welcomes whoever is interested in the topic of the speech.

（→名詞子句做受詞）

主辦人歡迎任何對這個演講議題有興趣的人來參加。

- He is kind to whoever comes to him for help.

（→名詞子句做受詞）

他對任何向他求助的人都很友善。

4. 疑問詞除了構成直接疑問句外，由疑問詞所引導的子句也可接在主要子句後面構成間接問句，這種子句為名詞子句，可做主詞、受詞或補語。

- <u>Who will win the biggest prize</u> is still unknown.

（→名詞子句做主詞）

誰會得到最大獎仍是未知。

- I asked the customer <u>what he would order.</u>（→名詞子句做受詞）

我問客人要點什麼菜。

- The question was <u>when we could get there.</u>（→名詞子句做主詞補語）

問題就是我們何時能到達那邊。

3.「疑問副詞」引導之名詞子句

疑問副詞是用來詢問訊息的副詞，包括how（如何、怎麼樣）、when（何時）、where（何地）、why（為什麼）。這一類名詞子句的結構為疑問副詞＋直述句，或稱為間接問句。

- **The client asks me when the goods will be delivered.**
  （→名詞子句做直接受詞）
  我的顧客問我貨物何時會運送。

- **Let's take a close look at how bees collect pollen.**
  （→名詞子句做受詞）
  讓我們近一點看蜜蜂如何蒐集花粉。

- **However, when people send flowers may be different across different cultures.**
  （→名詞子句做主詞）
  然而，人們何時送花會因文化而不同。

4.「疑問代名詞」引導之名詞子句

疑問代名詞為疑問詞＋代名詞，包括who（誰—主詞）、whom（誰—受詞）、what（什麼）、which（哪一個）、whose（誰的—所有格）。在這一種名詞子句裡，因為疑問代名詞代替了子句裡的主詞或受詞，所以結構為疑問代名詞＋不完整子句（缺S或O）。

- **No one can predict what will happen next.**
  （→名詞子句做直接受詞）
  沒有人能預測接下來會發生什麼。

- **We are not sure whom the baggage belongs to.**
  （→名詞子句做同位語）
  我們沒辦法確定這個行李是屬於誰的。

- **No words would be necessary to know what the foreigner meant.**
  （→名詞子句做直接受詞）
  不需言語就可以明白那位外國人的意思。

- **To prove their point, they cited a study about what might influence a person's choice of career path.** （→名詞子句做補語）
  為了證明他們的論點，他們引用了一篇研究說明什麼會影響一個人的職涯選擇。

- Could you tell me <u>whose film was the most popular one among teenagers?</u>（→名詞子句做直接受詞）
  你可以告訴我誰的電影最受青少年歡迎嗎？

5. 名詞子句與不定詞片語之轉換

　　當主要子句的主詞和疑問副詞／疑問代名詞引導的子句主詞相同時，常用不定詞片語來替換。原本的名詞子句為疑問詞＋子句，替換後則變成疑問詞＋to＋原形動詞。

- I don't know what I should say.
  = I don't know what to say.
  （→去掉名詞子句內的I should，保留主要動詞say）
  我不知道（我）該說什麼。

- You'll know how you should operate the machine as long as you read the manual.
  = You'll know how to operate the machine as long as your read the manual.（→去掉名詞子句內的I should，保留主要動詞operate）
  只要你閱讀手冊，（你）就會知道該怎麼操作機器。

Test ➤快來即時測驗自己的學習成果吧！

( ) 1. I wonder _____ the chef used to season the turkey.
　　(A) that　　(B) whether　　(C) whatever　　(D) what

( ) 2. _____ breaks the traffic rules will have to take the penalty.
　　(A) Whether　　(B) Whoever　　(C) Whatever　　(D) That

( ) 3. Jenny believes in _____ her parents told her.
　　(A) that　　(B) which　　(C) whoever　　(D) whatever

( ) 4. He is not sure _____ his client will arrive.
　　(A) what　　(B) which　　(C) when　　(D) if

( ) 5. Jessica didn't tell me _____ book she was reading.
　　(A) whether　　(B) whose　　(C) that　　(D) where

解答：(D) (B) (D) (C) (B)

Part **2** | 副詞子句

 **1. 副詞子句的類型**

　　從屬連接詞所引導的子句，稱為副詞子句。其文法作用與副詞相同，副詞子句最常修飾主要子句中的時間與因果，可置於句首、句中、句尾。

1. 副詞子句的種類

　　❶ 表時間的副詞連接詞

　　❷ 表原因／結果的副詞連接詞

　　❸ 表讓步的副詞連接詞

　　❹ 表條件的副詞連接詞

　　❺ 表目的的副詞連接詞

　　❻ 表對比／相反的副詞連接詞

2. 副詞子句的連接詞

　　❶ 表時間：before, after, by the time, as, while, when, whenever, until, since, during, as soon as

　　❷ 表條件：if, unless, in case of/that, as long as, in case that

　　❸ 表原因：because, since, as, because of, now that, due to, owing to

　　❹ 表目的：lest, in order to/that, so that

　　❺ 表結果：so/such... that

　　❻ 表讓步：although, though, despite, in spite of, even if, even though

 **2. 各種副詞子句**

1. 表「時間」之副詞子句：

　　表「時間」之副詞子句，是指以when（當）、while（當）、whenever（每當）、since（自從）、after（在……之後）、before（在……之前）、during（在……期間）、until（直到）、as（當）、by the time（在……的時候）、as soon as（一……就）等詞所引導的完整子句。

- I always review the lessons before <u>I take a test</u>.
  我總是在考試前複習課業。

- He visited many tourist spots when <u>he traveled to Europe</u>.
  他去歐洲旅行時參觀了許多旅遊景點。

- She has been living in the mansion since <u>she inherited it from her uncle</u>.
  她自從繼承了叔叔的豪宅之後就一直住在裡面。

- As soon as <u>the siren went off</u>, people rushed out of the building.
  警報一響，人們就趕著離開這棟建築物。

- I was working on my report as <u>the earthquake hit last night</u>.
  昨晚地震發生時，我正在做報告。

2. 表「條件」之副詞子句

　　表「條件」之副詞子句，是以if（如果）、as long as（只要）、unless（除非）、in case of（萬一）等詞所引導的完整子句。

- We won't go hiking if it rains tomorrow.
  如果明天下雨，我們就不會去健行了。

- If you can't attend the class today, inform your tutor in advance.
  如果今天你無法上課，要事先通知你的家教老師。

- We can complete the project as long as we all work together.
  只要我們大家合作，就可以完成這個計畫。

- You can't win the trust of others unless you show your sincerity.
  如果沒有展現出誠意，是無法贏得他人信任的。

3. 表「原因」之副詞子句

表「原因」之副詞子句，是以because（因為）、since（由於、既然）、as（因為）、because of（因為）、now that（既然）、due to（由於）、owning to（由於）等詞所引導的完整子句。

- **Mom told me to avoid any food with peanuts as I am allergic to it.**
  媽媽告訴我要避免任何有花生的食物，因為我會過敏。

- **People in the country suffered from famine when there was scarce produce during the drought.**
  這個國家的人們因為乾旱期間缺乏糧食而遭受飢荒之苦。

- **Since you are not familiar with the corporate culture yet, you had better follow the example of the veteran worker.**
  既然你還不熟悉企業文化，最好就先遵循資深員工的先例。

- **Making a presentation in English was a piece of cake for John because he is a proficient speaker of the language .**
  用英文做簡報對約翰來說易如反掌，因為他的英文很流利。

4. 表「目的」之副詞子句：

表「目的」之副詞子句，是以in order to（為了）、so that（為了……而）、lest（以免）等詞所引導的完整子句。

- **The host of the event prepared a lot of candies so that every child attending the party can get one.**
  主持人準備了很多糖果，為了讓每個參加派對的小孩都可以拿到一個。

- **The company asked the employees not to use their smartphone in the office so that they could be more focused at work.**
  這間公司要求員工在辦公室內不要使用智慧型手機以便他們能專心工作。

目的若為完整的句子，則用in order that或so that連接兩個動作，但此時in order不可省略；so that不可置於句首！

- **The factory owner applied for a loan in order that he could upgrade the production line.**

  = The factory owner applied for a loan so that he could upgrade the production line.

  = So that he could upgrade the production line, the factory owner applied for a loan.

5. 表「結果」之副詞子句

表「結果」之副詞子句，是以so (such) ... that（太……所以）等詞所引導的完整子句。

- Yvonne is so shy that <u>she avoided any chance to speak to strangers.</u>
  伊芳非常害羞，所以她避免任何和陌生人說話的機會。
- The client was so satisfied with our product that he placed an order right away.
  顧客對我們的產品很滿意，所以立刻就下訂單。
- The old man was so weak that he couldn't speak normally.
  老人是如此虛弱，以至於不能正常地說話。
- Jerry is such a lousy person that he couldn't even keep his desk clean.
  傑瑞是如此邋遢，連保持書桌乾淨也做不到。

6. 表「讓步」之副詞子句：

表「讓步」之副詞子句，是以although、though、despite、in spite of、even if、even though（皆為儘管、即使之意）等詞所引導的完整子句。

- Although he has a tight schedule, he manages to attend a culinary class after work every Wednesday.
  雖然他行程很滿，他還是挪出時間每個星期三下班後去上一堂烹飪課。
- Even though the company is rather small, it can make a lot of profit.
  儘管這間公司很小，它還是賺了很多利潤。
- Gina purchased the craft as a souvenir even though it is not very practical.
  吉娜買了一個手工藝品作為紀念品，雖然它不怎麼實用。
- Gary likes to play with Lego bricks although he is only 3 years old.
  蓋瑞雖然才三歲，卻喜歡玩樂高積木。

( ) 1. Kevin completed the project _____ he didn't get support from his colleagues.

(A) since   (B) even though   (C) so that   (D) for

( ) 2. The store adopted a new POS system _____ it can save customers' time.

(A) because of   (B) although   (C) so that   (D) rather than

( ) 3. The football game was put off _____ the heavy rain.

(A) because of   (B) since   (C) while   (D) although

( ) 4. The event will be held as scheduled _____ the organizer was asked to cancel it by the government.

(A) so that   (B) due to   (C) unless   (D) ever since

( ) 5. We will continue with the project _____ our supervisor approves it.

(A) despite   (B) unless   (C) because   (D) as long as

解答：(B) (C) (A) (C) (D)

Note

　　此句型為主詞＋（不及物）動詞的形式，動詞本身不需要加上受詞和補語，即能表達完整意思，也常與地方副詞、時間副詞、情狀副詞等連用，使句意更加完整。

- <u>It</u> <u>rained</u> <u>heavily</u> <u>in northern Taiwan</u> <u>yesterday.</u>
  S + Vi. ＋ 情狀副詞 ＋ 地方副詞 ＋時間副詞
  昨天北台灣雨下得很大。

- <u>She</u> <u>cried</u> <u>very loudly</u> <u>last night.</u>
  S ＋ Vi. ＋ 情狀物詞 ＋ 時間副詞
  她昨晚哭得很大聲。

- <u>The lecturer</u> <u>speaks</u> <u>passionately</u> <u>on the stage.</u>
  S ＋ Vi. ＋ 情狀副詞 ＋ 地方副詞
  講者在台上激動地演說。

- <u>Time</u> <u>flies</u> <u>like an arrow</u> and <u>waits</u> for <u>no man.</u>
  S. ＋ Vi. ＋ 情狀副詞 ＋ Vi ＋ 受詞
  光陰似箭、歲月不饒人。

- <u>Hundreds of people</u> <u>participated</u> in the event <u>on Thanksgiving Day.</u>
  S ＋. Vi. ＋ 時間副詞
  數百人在感恩節參加這個活動。

- <u>We</u> must <u>start</u> out <u>early</u> to get good bargains in the sale <u>tomorrow.</u>
  S. ＋ Vi. ＋ 情狀副詞 ＋ 時間副詞
  為了在拍賣時買到好東西，我們明天要早點出發。

- How will <u>we</u> <u>get</u> <u>there</u> <u>tomorrow morning</u>?
  S ＋ Vi ＋ 地方副詞 ＋ 時間副詞

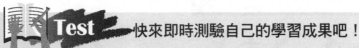

( ) 1. The client will _____ the venue at 2 o'clock this afternoon.
    (A) arrive   (B) arrive at   (C) come   (D) go

( ) 2. Judy often _____ music on her headphones when she takes the bus.
    (A) hear   (B) hear to   (C) listens   (D) listens to

( ) 3. The customer service representative is _____ the phone.
    (A) speaking   (B) talking
    (C) speaking on   (D) talking in

( ) 4. Mandy _____ Europe last summer. She visited several countries there.
    (A) traveled   (B) went
    (C) traveled around   (D) went by

( ) 5. The lease will _____ at the end of the month.
    (A) affect   (B) expire   (C) practice   (D) implement

解答：(B) (D) (C) (C) (B)

Note

　　此為主詞＋（不及物）動詞＋主詞補語的結構；用來補充說明主詞狀態者，稱為主詞補語（SC），形式有名詞、形容詞、分詞、片語、子句……等。此句型有兩大適用的動詞類別：

1. be 動詞

● He is an engineer.
　他是一位工程師。

● To see is to believe.
　百聞不如一見／眼見為憑。

2. 連綴動詞

　　(1) 似乎動詞：seem, look, appear

　　(2) 保持動詞：keep, remain, stay, continue

　　(3) 來去動詞：go, come, return

　　(4) 站坐動詞：sit, lie, stand

　　(5) 變成動詞：go, run, get, turn, grow, fall, become

　　(6) 感官動詞：see, look, sound, smell, taste, feel

● The kid seems very disappointed.（S.C. 為形容詞）
　S　　+V +　　　　　S.C.
　小朋友似乎很失望。

● The water seemed very clean.（S.C. 為形容詞）
　　S　　　+V　　+ S.C.
　水似乎很乾淨。

● The milk went sour.（S.C. 為形容詞）
　　S.　+V + S.C.
　牛奶壞掉了。

- Good advice is harsh to the ears. （S.C. 為形容詞）
  　　　　S 　　 + V 　　 + S.C.
  忠言逆耳。

- The theme is how women break the glass ceiling at workplace.
  （S.C. 為名詞片語）
  　　　S. 　 + V 　 + S.C.
  主題是女性如何打破職場的升遷限制。

- The clock is ticking. （S.C. 為現在分詞）
  　　S 　 + V + S.C.
  時間正在流逝。

- The mails from advertisers will be sent to the folder of spams.
  （S.C. 為過去分詞）
  　　S 　　　　　　　　　　　　　 + V + S.C.
  廣告商寄來的郵件會被放置到垃圾郵件資料夾裡。

Test 快來即時測驗自己的學習成果吧！

( ) 1. The music sounds _____.
  (A) please 　　(B) pleased 　　(C) pleasing 　　(D) pleasure

( ) 2. George _____ his report when I called on him.
  (A) was working on 　(B) modifies 　(C) made changes 　(D) revise

( ) 3. Mary _____ for more than eight hours yesterday.
  (A) bought 　　(B) slept 　　　(C) changed 　　(D) went

( ) 4. The students _____ still when the principal was speaking.
  (A) look 　　　(B) stand 　　　(C) sat 　　　(D) seem

( ) 5. She appeared _____ while we were rehearsing for the play.
  (A) tiring 　　(B) exhausted 　(C) merrily 　(D) generously

解答：(C) (A) (B) (C) (B)

112

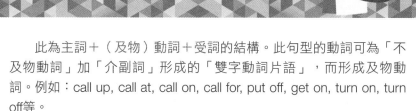

Chapter3 子句與五大句型

Part 5 | S + V + O

　　此為主詞＋（及物）動詞＋受詞的結構。此句型的動詞可為「不及物動詞」加「介副詞」形成的「雙字動詞片語」，而形成及物動詞。例如：call up, call at, call on, call for, put off, get on, turn on, turn off等。

● We must protect the environment.
　　S. +助動詞 + V + O （→受詞為名詞）
　　我們必須保護環境。

● I didn't know what to say.
　　S. + V + O （→受詞為名詞片語）
　　我不知道該説什麼。

● He enjoys playing online games with his friends.
　　S. + V + O （→受詞為動名詞）
　　他喜歡和朋友玩線上遊戲。

● He thinks that he has made a good investment.
　　S. + V + O （→受詞為名詞子句）
　　他認為他做了很好的投資。

● Jerry treats the rich and the poor equally.
　　S. + V + O + 副詞 （→受詞為複數名詞）
　　傑瑞平等地對待富人和窮人。

● My roommate and I take turns cleaning the bathroom and the kitchen.
　　S. + V + O （→受詞為動名詞片語）
　　我的室友和我輪流打掃浴室和廚房。

( ) 1. 下列何者為S+V+O的句型？

(A) Kevin cooks dinner for his family.

(B) Simon exercises every day.

(C) Nancy never cries in front of others.

(D) Mile laughs loudly.

( ) 2. Tom never put off _____ document required by his supervisor.

(A) hand in   (B) printed   (C) submitting   (D) to give

( ) 3. Global warming has _____ many severe problems in different countries.

(A) resulted   (B) brought   (C) led   (D) caused

( ) 4. The nurses will _____ the wounded and the ill.

(A) attend   (B) take care of   (C) show concern   (D) being medicine

( ) 5. I think _____.

(A) to change my schedule

(B) putting off the event

(C) what to say

(D) that money can't buy ture love

解答：(A) (C) (D) (B) (D)

114

Part 6 | S+V+IO+DO

　　此為主詞＋（及物）動詞＋間接受詞＋直接受詞的結構，為授與動詞用法，其後需接兩個受詞：一為直接受詞（DO），通常為物，另一為間接受詞（IO），通常為人。若間接受詞（IO）與直接受詞（DO）對調，則應加上適當的介系詞。

★ **常用的授與動詞包括：**

授與動詞			介系詞
pay（付）	tell（告訴）	bring（帶來）	
give（給）	sell（賣）	deliver（遞送）	to
lend（借給）	teach（教）	show（指示）	
send（寄給）	write（寫給）	offer（提供）	
buy（買）	order（訂購）	choose（選擇）	for
make（做）	get（取得）	leave（留給）　sing（唱）	
ask（要求、問）　inquire（要求）　make（做）			of
play（開玩笑）			on

- She played a trick on me.
   　S　+ V + DO + 介系詞 +IO
  = She played me a trick.
   　S + 　V + 　IO + DO 　（→DO 為名詞）
  她開了我一個玩笑。

- My grandmother made a cake for me.
   　　 S　+ 　　 V + DO + 介系詞 +IO
  = My grandmother made me a cake.
   　S + V + IO + DO 　（→DO 為名詞）
  我的外婆做了一個蛋糕給我。

- My friend showed a special photo to me.
  S ＋ V ＋ DO + 介系詞 ＋IO

  = My friend showed me a special photo.
  S + V + IO + DO （→DO 為名詞）
  我的朋友給我看一張特別的照片。

- Kevin asked a personal question of me.
  S ＋ V ＋ DO + 介系詞 ＋IO

  = Kevin asked me a personal question.
  S + V + IO + DO （→DO 為名詞）
  凱文問我一個私人的問題。

- The veteran worker taught me how to operate the machine.
  S + V ＋ IO + DO （→DO 為名詞片語）
  資深職員教我如何操作機器。

- The secretary told us that the meeting will be postponed to next week.
  S + V + IO + DO （→DO 為名詞子句）
  秘書告訴我們這次會議將會延到下個星期。

Test — 快來即時測驗自己的學習成果吧！

( ) 1. Reading can _____ you a lot of benefit.
  (A) show　　(B) bring　　(C) leave　　(D) lend

( ) 2. The good will _____ the client by next Friday.
  (A) be delivered to　　(B) deliver
  (C) be brought about　　(D) bring

( ) 3. The old lady weaved a scarf _____ her grandson.
  (A) to　　(B) of　　(C) on　　(D) for

( ) 4. 選出正確的句子。
  (A) Michael wrote his girlfriend a song.
  (B) Terry told a joke his friends.
  (C) The interviewer asked an inappropriate question to her.
  (D) Betty taught his students.

( ) 5. My friend _____ a ticket to Mayday's concert.
  (A) got me　　(B) played on me　　(C) made for me　　(D) wrote me

解答：(B) (A) (D) (A) (A)

Part **7** | S + V + O + O.C.

　　此為主詞＋（及物）動詞＋受詞＋受詞補語的結構，用來補充説明受詞狀態者，稱為受詞補語（OC），形式有名詞、形容詞、分詞、片語、子句……等。此句型的動詞有其特殊性質，類型如下：

1. 帶有認為受格具有某種狀態或某種性質的動詞，包括： think（想）、believe（相信）、find（發現）、consider（認為）等。

● I find my cousin very talented.
　　我發現我的表姊很有才華。

2. 帶有使受格進入某種狀態或某種性質的動詞，包括：make（使）、want（想要）、cut（切斷）、keep（守住）、leave（遺留）等。

● Don't leave the stove on.
　　V ＋ O ＋ OC　（→OC 為形容詞）
　　不要把爐子一直開著。

● We will keep the matter unpublicized.
　　S ＋ V ＋ O ＋ OC　（→OC 為形容詞）
　　我們不會公開這件事。

● Do you want your steak medium or well-done?
　　S ＋ V ＋ O ＋ O.C.　（→OC 為形容詞）
　　你想要牛排五分熟還是全熟呢？

3. 表示命名、稱作的動詞，後面出現的補語通常是名詞，包括：name（命名）、call（稱呼）、nickname（為……取小名）。

● We called him a walking encyclopedia.
　　S ＋ V ＋ O ＋ OC　（→OC 為名詞片語）
　　我們稱呼他為行走的百科全書。

- They name the polar bear cub Hertha.

  S + V + O + OC （→OC 為名詞）
  他們將這個北極熊寶寶命名為荷沙。

- We nicknamed her kitty for she was as tamed as a cat.

  S + V + O + OC （→OC 為名詞）
  我們暱稱她為凱蒂，因為她就像貓一樣溫馴。

- Mom told me to do the chores today.

  S + V + O + OC （→OC 為動詞片語）
  媽媽要我今天做家事。

- I heard Mandy yell at her son.

  S + V + O + OC （→OC 為動詞原型）
  我聽到曼蒂在對他的兒子大吼。

- She noticed a boy distributing flyers at the corner of the street.

  S + V + O + OC （→OC 為現在分詞）
  她注意到一個男孩在街角發傳單。

4. 表示認為……是的動詞，這些動詞後面的補語之前要先加as，包括：regard（把……看作）、treat（看待）、think of（認為）、look upon（視為）、refer to（認為）等。

- I think of her as the mentor of my life.

  S + V + O + OC （→OC 為名詞片語）
  我將她視為是我的人生導師。

- They treated the refugees like dirt.

  S + V + O + OC （→OC 為名詞）
  他們不把難民當人看。

- We refer to the scholar as an authority figure in this research field.

  S + V + O + OC （→OC 為現在）
  我們認為這位學者是這個研究領域的權威人士。

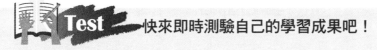

( ) 1. 下列何者不是S+V+O+OC 的句型。

(A) We view him as our model.

(B) Jerry lent us his new car.

(C) They regard the task as a difficult one.

(D) He had his hair cut yesterday.

( ) 2. Jerry _____ outdoor activities to be good for the kids' health.

(A) considers (B) regards (C) views (D) thinks of

( ) 3. They think with hard work, they could make their dream _____.

(A) come true (B) realizing

(C) into practice (D) to become reality

( ) 4. The employees were told to _____ the project secret.

(A) name (B) keep (C) want (D) regard

( ) 5. Mike used gestures, trying to make himself _____ by the foreigner.

(A) understand (B) understood

(C) understanding (D) to understand

解答：(B) (A) (A) (B) (B)

Note

( ) 1. The wounded soldier lay _____ on the stretcher, and the medical professionals are working hard to save him.
(A) dying   (B) treating   (C) healing   (D) curing

( ) 2. The teacher encourages students to _____ books from the library.
(A) give   (B) deliver   (C) borrow   (D) lend

( ) 3. The suspect remained _____ on the court.
(A) silence   (B) silent   (C) silently   (D) for silence

( ) 4. She found the teenager _____ the store with some goods without paying for them.
(A) to leave   B) leave   (C) left   (D) leaving

( ) 5. Helen brought a birthday cake _____ her mother.
(A) to   (B) for   (C) in   (D) on

( ) 6. He _____ ambition as a key factor for success.
(A) regards   (B) thinks   (C) considers   (D) looks

( ) 7. She regrets _____ the mean words to her classmates.
(A) she had said   (B) to say
(C) that has said   (D) having said

( ) 8. The newcomer appears rather _____.
(A) patience   (B) patiently
(C) friendly   (D) friendliness

( ) 9. Nick will have his car _____ this afternoon.
(A) repair   (B) to repair   (C) repairing   (D) repaired

( ) 10. The best way to build friendship with others is _____ shared interests.

(A) to find   (B) finds   (C) found   (D) in finding

( ) 11. Cindy _____ for one hour every day.

(A) visits   (B) exercises   (C) checks   (D) decides

( ) 12. Nancy asked her colleague _____ her a favor.

(A) to do   (B) of doing   (C) leave   (D) make

( ) 13. The haters on the Internet seemed rather _____ about the celebrity's latest post on the social network website.

(A) pleasant   (B) offending   (C) upset   (D) tiring

( ) 14. Only half of the interviewees knew _____ Taiwan is.

(A) that   (B) which   (C) such   (D) where

( ) 15. The stars shine _____ in the night sky.

(A) bright   (B) brightly   (C) brightness   (D) brighten

Chapter 4
常用句型

Part 1 | 對等比較句型
as...as...的用法

 1. 意思為「和……一樣」時

1. as...as...中第一個as為副詞，第二個as為連接詞。中間須接形容詞或副詞原級，或者是不定詞數量詞（如much、many、little等），視句子所要表達的意思而定。

2. 這個句型中，如果動詞為及物動詞，則形容詞與受詞須一起放在as...as...中間。

- To promote the new product, the sales representatives have to contact as many potential customers as possible.
  為了推廣新產品，業務代表要盡可能聯絡多一些潛在顧客。

- She is as old as I.
  = She and I are of the same age.
  她跟我同年。

- It is as warm as it was yesterday.
  今天跟昨天一樣溫暖。

- The electronic cooker is as useful a gadget as the microwave oven.
  電鍋跟微波爐一樣是有用的工具。

- She doesn't visit her grandparents as often as she used to.
  她沒有像過去一樣常常拜訪祖父母了。

- In order to keep up with the fast-changing society, you should expose yourself to as much information as possible.
  為了跟上快速變遷的社會，你應該盡量多接觸一些資訊。

由as...as衍生出來的兩個常用句型

1. as long as或so long as，有三種句意

❶ 一樣

- My purse is as expensive as yours.
  我的皮包跟你的一樣貴。

❷ 只要

- The expert says that the one-time surgical mask can be reused as long as it is properly cleaned.
  專家說只要醫療口罩有適當地清潔就可以重複使用。

❸ 長達

- He was confined in the hospital for as long as three months.
  他住院長達三個月的時間。

2. as far as或so far as，有三種句意

❶ 一樣遠

- The distance from here to the convenience store is as far as to the vending machine.
  從這裡到便利商店的距離就和到販賣機的距離一樣遠。

❷ 就……而言

- So far as I have heard, the owner of the grocery store is the most generous person in the community.
  就我所知，雜貨店老闆是社區裡面最慷慨的人。

❸ 遠至

- The marathon runner ran as far as he could, but he failed to reach the goal in the end.
  馬拉松跑者盡可能跑遠一點，但是沒能夠跑到終點。

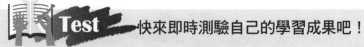

( ) 1. Janet can sing _____ professional singer.

    (A) as good as   (B) as well as   (C) as far as   (D) as long as

( ) 2. The test questions are _____ as those in the quiz.

    (A) so easy as   (B) as easy as   (C) so easily that (D) as easily that

( ) 3. _____ I could can think of, this is the most practical proposal.

    (A) As long as   (B) As far as   (C) As long as   (D) As old as

( ) 4. Kevin worked _____ most of his coworkers but he receives a lower salary.

    (A) hardly as   (B) less hardly   (C) as hard as   (D) hard as

( ) 5. Helen can complete the report in time _____ her colleagues gives her a hand.

    (A) as many as   (B) as far as

    (C) as much as   (D) as long as

解答：(B) (A) (B) (C) (D)

Note

126

Part 2 | The adj.-er..., the adj.-er... 「越⋯⋯就越⋯⋯」

屬於條件句用法，此時句型的前半句用簡單現在式，而後半句用未來式。

- **The faster you run, the better chance you have to win the race.**
  你跑得越快，就越有機會贏得賽跑。

- **The more goods you sell, the more incentive bonus you may get.**
  你賣越多商品，就會得到越多的獎金。

- **The more haste, the less speed.**
  欲速則不達。

- **The more one knows, the more ignorant he finds himself.**
  一個人知道得越多，就越覺得自己無知。

- **The more work experience you have, the more sophisticated you'll become.**
  你的工作經驗越多，就會越成熟。

- **The higher you climb, the farther you see.**
  爬得越高，看得越遠。

- **The higher the purity of gold is, the more valuable it is.**
  黃金的純度越高，就越有價值。

- **The older he becomes, the wiser he gets.**
  隨著他年紀漸增，他也越來越有智慧。

- **The longer you work here, the more familiar you are with the work.**
  你在這裡工作越久，就對工作越熟悉。

- **The more money you spend on the luxuries, the less likely you are able to save money.**
  你在奢侈品上花越多錢，就越不可能存到錢。

( ) 1. The _____ hasty you get, the more mistake you may make.

(A) more   (B) less   (C) as   (D) so

( ) 2. The _____ you make, the more important it is to manage your finance well.

(A) less work   (B) more money   (C) fewer mistakes   (D) more time

( ) 3. The _____ she speaks, the less understandable her speech is.

(A) fast   (B) more fast   (C) fastest   (D) faster

( ) 4. The _____ you stay in the hospital, the higher risk you have to contract disease.

(A) farther   (B) longer   (C) sooner   (D) less

( ) 5.The sooner they arrive, the _____ we can start the meeting.

(A) earlier   (B) longer   (C) farther   (D) latest

解答：(A) (B) (D) (B) (A)

Note

Part **3** | 倍數比較法

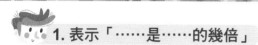 **1. 表示「……是……的幾倍」**

句型：S＋V＋（1. 倍數用法）＋（2. 比較用法）

倍數+比較級+than

倍數+as + adj. (+N) + as …

倍數+the + N + of …

1. 倍數用法

❶ 小數

0.5 ： half

1 ： as adj. as

1.5 ： one time and a half

2 ： two times

2.5 ： two times and a half

❷ 分數

1/2 ： half

1/3 ： one-third

2/3 ： two-thirds

3/4 ： three fourths

2 比較用法：as + adj. + as + the + N + of

大：large = the size of

小：small = the size of

長：long = the length of

短：short = the length of

數：many = the number of

量：much = the amount of

快：fast = the speed of

慢：slow = the speed of

深：deep = the depth of

淺：shallow = the depth of

寬：wide = the width of

窄：narrow = the width of

遠：far = the distance of

近：near = the distance of

高：tall　= the height of

矮：short = the height of

胖：fat = the weight of

瘦：thin = the weight of

輕：light = the weight of

重：heavy = the weight of

長：old = the age of

幼：young = the age of

3 其他用法

❶ half as（many/much/old/long）...as... （……的一半）

❷ half as（many/much/old/long）...again as... （……的一倍半）

❸ again as（many/much/old/long）...as... （……的兩倍）

❹ X as（many/much/old/long）...again as... （……的兩倍）

- **My apartment is half as large as yours.**
  我的公寓是你的一半。

- **My apartment is half as large again as yours.**
  我的公寓是你的一倍半

- **My apartment is as large again as yours.**
  我的公寓是你的兩倍。

- **The diamond ring is three times as expensive as the golden ring.**
  = The diamond ring is three times the price of the golden ring.
  = The diamond ring is three times more expensive than the golden ring.
  鑽戒是金戒指的三倍貴。

- **The opponent is so strong that he had to fight twice as hard as he used to do to win in the competition.**
  對手如此強勁，他必須要比以前努力兩倍才能贏得比賽。

- **The amount of time I spent on communicating with the customer is one third of an hour. That is, it took me twenty minutes to talk with the customer.**
  我花了三分之一個小時的時間跟這位客人溝通。也就是說，我花了二十分鐘和這位客人講話。

- **Only half of the students participate in the graduation trip.**
  只有一半的學生參加了這次的畢業旅行。

Test 快來即時測驗自己的學習成果吧！

( ) 1. Mandy spent _____ I did on buying the apron.
  (A) half the price   (B) half as many as
  (C) so expensive as   (D) two times as much

( ) 2. The smartphone is _____ of the traditional cellphone.
  (A) as heavy   (B) the weight   (C) have as heavy   (D) half the weight

( ) 3. Their classroom is _____ as ours. That is, their classroom is 1.5 times the size of our classroom.
  (A) one and half again   (B) twice the size
  (C) as large   (D) twice larger

( ) 4. Taking the subway to our destination takes thirty minutes, while taking the bus takes _____. That is, it takes about one hour to go there by bus.
  (A) twice long   (B) two time longer
  (C) twice as long   (D) two times as

( ) 5. Mr. Wang was _____ when he taught us history back in high school days.
  (A) twice as old   (B) twice my age   (C) two times old   (D) twice older

解答：(B) (A) (D) (C) (A)

131

Part 4 | more與less的用法

1. more 與 less 的基本用法

用法	中譯
more than	多餘、非常
less than	少於、很不
more A than B less B than A	1. 多／少於 2. 與其說A不如說B

- She is more than willing to help the stray dogs.
  她非常樂意幫助流浪狗。

- The sales figure last season is less than satisfying to the manager.
  經理覺得上一季銷售數字十分不理想。

- She is more a medicine peddler than a medical practitioner.
  與其說她是醫療人員，不如說她是賣藥的人。

- He has been less a problem solver than an eloquent negotiator.
  與其說他是問題解決者，不如說他是能言善道的斡旋者。

- Jack is known less as an illusionist than as a magician.
  傑克與其說是一個幻術師，更不如說是個魔術師。

2. more 和 less 的替換用法

no more than = only

no less than = as many/much as

not more than = at most

not less than = at least

中譯：跟……一樣少；只有跟……一樣多；多達至多

- What we could offer is no more than some daily necessities.
  我們只能夠提供一些日常用品。

- Busy as he is, he would spend at least one hour accompanying his little daughter every day.
  儘管他很忙，他每天還是會花至少一個小時陪伴他的小女兒。

- Since we have a tight budget for organizing the conference, we will not offer refreshments for the attendees.
  由於我們籌辦研討會的經費很有限，我們就不會提供與會者小點心。

- The researchers decided to recruit no fewer than 100 questionnaire respondents for the study.
  研究者決定至少要招募一百名問卷填答者。

 3. more 和 less 的延伸用法

用法	中譯
no more A than B	A 和 B 一樣→都不
no less A than B	A 和 B 一樣→都是

- The election campaign candidate is no more convincing than his opponent.
  這個選舉候選人和他的對手都一樣沒有說服力。

- She is as stubborn as a mule.
  她和驢子一樣固執。

用法	中譯
nothing more than	僅僅、只不過
nothing less than	簡直就是

- This story is nothing more than a slice of fake news.
  這個故事不過就是則假新聞。

- If he had not got the 20 points in the game, our team couldn't have won. He is nothing less than a game changer.
  他得到20分，我們的隊伍才能贏得比賽。他簡直就是扭轉了局勢。

( ) 1. Peter is _____ a hypocrite. He never means what he says on social occasions.
(A) nothing less than
(B) nothing more than
(C) no less than
(D) more than

( ) 2. We could allow _____ 100 visitors into the museum at once.
(A) no more than (B) less than (C) as much as (D) more than

( ) 3. She is _____ a con artist than a negotiator.
(A) as much (B) nothing less than (C) much (D) more

( ) 4. The discount during the sale will be _____ 5 percent. That is, you need to pay no more than 95 dollars for an one-hundred dollar item.
(A) no more than
(B) nothing more than
(C) no less than
(D) nothing less than

( ) 5. She is _____ an amateur performer _____ a professional musician. She just plays music for fun.
(A) more; than
(B) less; than
(C) nothing more; than
(D) nothing less; than r

Note

Part 5 「與其說是A， 不如說是B的句型」

1. 句型結構

> S+ V + so much as B = S + V + more B than A
>
> = S + V + not A so much as B = S + V + B instead of A
>
> = S + V + less A than B = S + V + B rather than A

- He is not so much an artist as a painting craftsman.

  = He is not an artist so much as a painting craftsman.

  = He is less an artist than a painting craftsman.

  = He is more a painting craftsman than an artist.

  = He is a painting craftsman rather than an artist.

  = He is a painting craftsman instead of an artist.

  與其說他是藝術家，不如說是畫匠。

- A man's virtue should be measured not so much by what he says as by what he does.

  我們與其從一個人說的話來判斷他的德性，不如從他做的事。

- The influence of an organization lies not so much on the size of its staff as on the strategies it takes.

  一個組織的影響力，與其說視它的規模而定，不如說視它的策略而定。

2. 連……都不（甚至……）的句型

> S+ 助V/beV not so much as ＋VR/adj./N
>
> → S＋have not so much as＋V-p.p.
>
> → S＋V＋without so much as＋V-ing

- After he went bankrupt, he could not support himself. He could not so much as afford a decent meal.

  破產之後，他無法養活自己。他甚至無法吃一餐正常的飯。

- My grandparents are illiterate. They could not so much as read the subtitles of the TV drama.

  我的祖父母不識字。他們連電視劇的字幕都無法讀懂。

- The owner of the deli cook the vegetables without so much as cleansing them beforehand, and the diners were astonished.

  小吃攤老闆沒有清洗蔬菜就把它們拿去煮，用餐的客人嚇呆了。

Test —快來即時測驗自己的學習成果吧！

( ) 1. 與其說他是一位教師，不如說他是一位演員。（選出正確的說法）

    (A) He is not so much an actor as a teacher.

    (B) He is less an actor than a teacher.

    (C) He is not so much a teacher as an actor.

    (D) He is more like a teacher than an actor.

( ) 2. The rube boy took away my umbrella _____ asking for permission.

    (A) without so much as   (B) instead of

    (C) not so much as   (D) less than

( ) 3. He is a _____ a guardian than a supervisor. He seldom gives instructions, but shows a lot of care for us.

    (A) more than   (B) less than

    (C) more   (D) less

( ) 4. He has difficulty talking to strangers. He could not _____ say a complete sentence when he is nervous.

    (A) very much   (B) so much as

    (C) as much as   (D) instead of

( ) 5. She was so tired that she went to sleep without _____ taking a shower.

    (A) more than   (B) rather than   (C) as many as   (D) so much as

解答：(C) (A) (C) (B) (D)

136

Part **6** 其他強調語句的比較級用法

1. 強調句型的比較級用法

> S＋V＋the last＋(N)＋to VR
>
> 「絕非、最不可能……」+ that 子句

- He is the last candidate to be shortlisted for the final round of interview.
  他是最不可能入選到最終面試的候選人。

- The falling stock price was the last thing that we had expected.
  股價下跌是我們最預料不到的事情。

2. 用adv.＋比較級來強調「更不用說、更何況」

> 肯定句＋much more＋N
>
> 否定句＋much less＋N

- The drugstore sells hand sanitizer and forehead thermometer, much more medical masks.
  這間藥局販賣乾洗手和額溫槍，更別說常用的口罩了。

- She doesn't like sausage and ham, much less pork.
  她不喜歡香腸和火腿，更別說是豬肉了。

2. 比較級的修飾種類

> ❶ very/really/so...＋原級
>
> ❷ far/much/even/still/a lot/a little/a great deal＋比較級
>
> ❸ the very/much the/by far the＋最高級

- Matt works very hard.
  麥特非常努力。

- Matt works much harder than his colleagues.
  麥特比同事努力得多。

- Matt works by far the hardest among all workers in the company.
  在所有員工當中，麥特是最努力的。
- James is the very most creative chef that I have ever known.
  = James is much the most creative chef that I have ever known.
  = James is by far the most creative chef that I have ever known.
  詹姆士是我認識最有創意的主廚。

3. 以more/less的句型強調「更加、更不」

相關片語列表：

❶ all the more （更加）

❷ all the less （更不）

❸ none the more（沒有比較好=一樣）

❹ none the less（沒有比較差=一樣）

- I am all the more nervous because the deadline of the report is approaching.
  我感到更緊張了，因為報告的截止期限就快到了。

- The time he devoted was all the less worthwhile because the job could be done more efficiently with the assistance of artificial intelligence.
  他投入的時間根本不值得，因為這個工作可以由人工智慧協助更有效力地去完成。

- He is none the less energetic although he stayed up late last night.
  雖然他昨晚熬夜，還是很有精神。

- He is none the happier because he was awarded the best actor award.
  他沒有因為贏得最佳男主角獎而更高興。

Test 快來即時測驗自己的學習成果吧!

( ) 1. He is _____ although he takes in a lot of supplementary foods.
   (A) none the healthier   (B) all healthier
   (C) no less heathier   (D) not the less healthy

( ) 2. Thomas is _____ the earnest researcher that I have met.
   (A) much more   (B) non the less   (C) a great deal   (D) by far

( ) 3. Her proposal was _____ practicable than ours. Bothe of the plans sound feasible.
   (A) no more   (B) no less   (C) all the more   (D) none the less

( ) 4. Mandy is _____ to reveal the confidential information to our opponent.
   (A) none the less   (B) no more than
   (C) the last person   (D) all the more possible

( ) 5. She is good at analyzing test items, _____ getting high exam scores.
   (A) much more   (B) no less   (C) all the more   (D) none the less

解答：(A) (D) (D) (C) (A)

Note

Part 7 | 表「如此…以至於…」的句型

 1. so/such...that... 如此…以至於…及相關用法

1. 句型要點：

so（**adj.**＋冠詞＋**N**）that＋子句such（冠詞＋**adj.**＋**N**）that＋子句
= so...as to＋VR（原形動詞）
= such...as to＋VR（原形動詞）
= adj.＋enough＋to VR（原形動詞）

2. 若出現名詞為單數可數名詞時，要注意冠詞a/an的位置，判斷使用 so/such。

3. 若出現複數名詞或不可數名詞，要使用such。

4. 若名詞前面出現many/much/few/little修飾的話，要使用so。

● The bus driver was such an enthusiastic person that all passengers enjoyed the ride.

（→such＋冠詞＋adj.＋N＋that＋子句）

= The bus driver was so enthusiastic that all passengers enjoyed the ride.

（→so＋adj.＋冠詞＋N＋that ＋子句）

這位公車司機是如此熱情，所有的乘客都很享受這趟旅程。

● These are such difficult questions that no one could solve them so far.

（→such＋複數N＋that＋子句）

這些是如此困難的問題，目前為止還沒有人可以解決它們。

● She announced the news with such joy that it was like the best thing that happened to her in her life.

（→such＋不可數N＋that＋子句）

她如此高興地宣布這件事，就好像那是她人生當中最好的一件事情了。

- He spend so much time practicing singing that he finally won the champion in the singing contest.

（→so＋much＋不可數N＋that＋子句）

他花了這麼多時間練習唱歌，終於在歌唱比賽中得到冠軍。

- He paid so little attention to his personal hygiene that he always appear sloppy.

（→so＋little＋不可數N＋that＋子句）

他對個人衛生如此不在意，以至於總是看起來很邋遢。

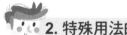 **2. 特殊用法的句型**

1. such與so的分別頗為類似感嘆句中what與how。

- It was such a gloom atmosphere that everyone remained silent for a while.

氣氛如此抑鬱，每個人都沈默了一陣子。

- She is such a peculiar child that she left a deep impression on me.
  = She is so peculiar a child that she left a deep impression on me.

她是如此特殊的孩子，以至於我對她印象很深刻。

2. so和such 都可以放在句首，但主要子句要倒裝。

- The clerk is so amiable that most shoppers like to chat with her.
  = Such amiable a person is the clerk that most shoppers like to chat with her.

  = So amiable is the clerk that most shoppers like to chat with her.

這位店員如此和藹可親，大部分顧客都喜歡和她聊天。

- I was so tired that I could hardly stay focused.
  = So tired was I that I could hardly stay focused.

我是如此疲倦，以至於無法保持專注。

3. such也可以用來替代某名詞，如果放在句首，後面主要子句要倒裝。

- Such was her anger that she lost her temper with the guest.

她是如此生氣以至於對客人發了脾氣。

• Such was the severe fire that all facilities in the factory were burned out.

那場大火如此嚴重，以至於工廠所有設備都燒毀了。

4. so...as to的用法

　　so...as to＋V的句型和so...that... 的句型相同，主要子句和從屬子句的主詞相同時，就可以改成so...as to＋V的句型。so...as to 表「如此……以至於……」，so as not to＋V表「為了不要……」。

• She keeps a frugal lifestyle so as to save money.
她過著節儉的生活，以便省錢。

• He avoids mentioning the bad memory so as not to make her feel sad. 他避免提到壞的回憶以免讓她感到傷心。

Test — 快來即時測驗自己的學習成果吧！

(　) 1. Helen was _____ a good salesperson _____ the company offers a high salary to keep her.

(A) so; that　　(B) such; that　　(C) so; as　　(D) so; as that

(　) 2. Kevin did _____ on the project _____ he got a big bonus.

(A) so well; that　　　　　(B) such good; that

(C) so well; as to　　　　　(D) such good; as

(　) 3. _____ that the leading actress became famous overnight.

(A) So popular the movie　　(B) The movie was such popular

(C) So popular a movie　　　(D) Such a popular movie it was

(　) 4. _____ that we could not proceed with our plan.

(A) We were in such dilemma　　(B) Such dilemma were we

(C) So a dilemma we were in　　　(D) Such was the dilemma we were

(　) 5. He left _____ that no one noticed that he was gone.

(A) such quietly　　　　　(B) such a quiet

(C) so quietly　　　　　　(D) so quiet

Part 8 | so that 的句型

1 表示「如此……以至於」的句型

So...as to + V 的句型和so...that 的句型型相同，主要子句和從屬子句的主詞相同時，就可以改成so...as to + V 的句型。so...as to表示「如此……以至於……」，so as not to + V 表示「為了不要……」。

- I am so naïve as to trust him.
  我是如此單純以至於相信他。

- Jerry is so tall that he can reach the top of the shelf.
  = Jerry is such a tall boy that he can reach the top of the shelf.
  = Jerry is so tall as to reach the top of the shelf.
  = Jerry is tall so as to reach the top of the shelf.
  傑瑞高得可以拿到架子頂端的東西。

- She appeared so confident that everyone at the meeting was convinced by her.
  = She appeared so confident as to convince everyone at the meeting.
  她是如此有自信，以至於會議上的每個人都被她說服了。

- He worked so hard that he would not be laid off.
  = He worked so hard as not to be laid off.
  他努力工作為了不要被裁員。

2 比較so as to的用法

so as to＋V = in order to＋V = so that＋cl.　表「為了」

- He edited his resume carefully so as to find a good job.
  = He edited his resume carefully in order to find a good job.
  = He edited his resume carefully so that he could find a good job.
  他小心地編輯履歷，為了找到一份好工作。

3 容易混淆的 so that 用法

so that 視其在句中的不同位置，會有不同的意義及用法

❶ 置於句中其前無逗點，表目的，中譯：為了 = in order that＋子句
❷ 置於句中其前有逗點，表結果，中譯：如此一來 = ; as a result, 子句
❸ 置於句首其前無逗點，表條件，中譯：只要 = as long as＋子句

- **Hank modified the document so that it could fulfill the company's requirement on the format.**
  (so that 置於句中，前面無逗點，表示目的)
  漢克修改文件以便讓它符合公司對格式的要求。

- **Exercise regularly, so that you can keep in shape.**
  (so that 的前面有逗點，表示結果) 規律運動，你就可以保持身材。

- **So that he covers for you, you can take a sick leave without worrying about the job. (so that 置於句首，前面無逗點，表示條件)**
  只要他幫你代班，你就可以請病假，不需要擔心工作。

Test — 快來即時測驗自己的學習成果吧！

( ) 1. We changed our schedule _____ meet the manager in town.
   (A) so that　　(B) so as to　　(C) in order that　　(D) for that

( ) 2. The PowerPoint slides were modified _____ they could be easier to understand for the conference attendees.
   (A) in order that　　(B) so as to　　(C) in order to　　(D) as long as

( ) 3. Berry revised her manuscript _____ the publisher would publish it for her.
   (A) as a result　　(B) in order to　　(C) in order to　　(D) so that

( ) 4. I was _____ stupid _____ make such mistakes.
   (A) so; in order that　　(B) so; that　　(C) so; as to　　(D) so; that

( ) 5. We had _____ limited time _____ we could not polish the language before submitting the report.
   (A) so; that　　(B) such; that　　(C) so; as to　　(D) such; that

144

Part 9 | cannot...too.../enough to.../too...to的用法

 1. cannot...too 再……也不為過

1. cannot...too表示「不可能太……；再……也不為過；應格外……；越……越好」，有下列四種變化，都表達同樣的意思。

❶ cannot＋V＋too much

❷ cannot over-V...

❸ cannot be too＋adj.

❹ cannot...enough （=cannot...sufficiently）

2. **not** 也可用其他否定副詞如 **never**、**hardly**、**scarcely** 來代替。

- You cannot be too careful when dealing with the accounting tasks.
  = You cannot be careful enough when dealing with the accounting tasks.
  你在處理會計事務的時候，再怎麼小心也不為過。

- We can never appreciate his kindness too much.
  = We can hardly appreciate his kindness enough.
  = We can scarcely appreciate his kindness sufficiently.
  我們再怎麼感謝他的善意都不為過。

- I cannot admire his courage too much.
  我非常欣賞他的勇氣。

- I cannot agree with you more.
  = I see eye to eye with you.
  我再同意你不過了。

3. cannot...too 與 cannot...over- 意思相同，常見的 over- 複合字包括：overemphasize（過分強調）、overestimate（高估）、overreact（過度反應）、overpraise（過度讚譽）等。

- We cannot overemphasize the importance of personal hygiene.
  個人衛生的重要性，再怎麼強調也不為過。

- We cannot overestimate the value of our cultural heritage.
  我們再怎麼高估文化遺產的價值也不為過。

2. adj./adv.＋enough to＋V 夠……而可以……

1. adj./adv.＋enough to 表示「夠……所以可以……」，此句型通常為：

S＋beV/V＋adj./adv.＋enough to＋V

2. adj./adv. + enough to + V 其實也可以代替成 so + adj. / adv. + as to + V

- Your son is old enough to take care of himself.
  你的兒子已經夠大，可以照顧他自己了。

- He does not look experienced enough to deal with the task by himself.
  他看起來不像有足夠經驗可以自己處理這件任務。

- He was eloquent enough to convince everybody to join the charity campaign.

  = He was so eloquent as to convince everybody to join the charity campaign.
  他口才夠好，可以說服大家參與這個慈善計畫。

- The lecturer talked logically enough to make herself understood by the audience.

  =The lecturer talked so logically as to make himself understood by the audience.
  講者說話邏輯很好，可以讓觀眾都了解他的意思。

1. enough除了修飾形容詞與副詞以外，也可修飾名詞。如果修飾名詞時，可置於名詞的前面或後面。

- He thinks he does not have enough time to develop any hobby.

  = He thinks he does not have time enough to develop any hobby.
  他覺得他沒有足夠的時間發展興趣。

- They didn't have enough medical resources to treat all of the patients.

  = They didn't have medical resources enough to treat all of the patients.
  他們沒有足夠的醫療資源救治所有的病患。

2. enough本身也可以做名詞使用。

- I have had enough of her negative emotions.
  我真的受夠了她的負面情緒了。

3. too...to 太……而不能……

1. too...to表示「太……而不能」，是否定用句型，有下列三種變化，都表達同樣的意思。

❶ too...to＋V

❷ too...for＋N

❸ too...for＋sb.＋to＋V

- Mandy is too weak to lift the box.
  曼蒂太虛弱了，搬不動這個箱子。

- The material is too fragile for making a container.
  這種材質太易碎了，不適合做容器。

- It was too cold for them to go swimming in the river.
  天氣太冷了，他們不要去河裡游泳比較好。

2. too...to＋V含有否定意思，但是請注意下列片語的意思。

● It is too easy to point finger on others when a mistake is revealed.
當錯誤被指出時，很容易就會責怪別人。（→too easy to表肯定）

● We were only too honored to be invited to the ceremony.
我們能受邀參加這個典禮，真是太榮幸了。（→only too...to表肯定）

● The man is too greedy not to ask for some rebate.
那個男子太貪心了，不可能不要求一些回扣。（→too...not to表肯定）

3. 除了too碰到單數名詞時，要把冠詞a/an 放在too＋adj.後面，其他像是so、as也是有這樣的用法。

● She is so meticulous a girl that she would check every document twice before submitting it.
她是如此細心的女孩，繳交所有文件之前都會檢查兩遍。

● He is as sophisticated as craftsman as you.
他和你一樣，都是很有經驗的工匠。

Test 快來即時測驗自己的學習成果吧！

( ) 1. We _____ when handling other's personal information.
    (A) cannot be too careful   (B) can be careful enough
    (C) can never be as careful   (D) can scarcely be careful

( ) 2. We _____ respect him _____ for his great achievement.
    (A) cannot; much   (B) can hardly; so much
    (C) cannot; too much   (D) could; enough

( ) 3. We _____ the importance of moral virtue.
    (A) can never overemphasize   (B) can overestimate
    (C) could overestimate   (D) could scarcely be estimated

( ) 4. I cannot admire his adventurous spirit _____.
    (A) scarcely   (B) hardly   (C) so much   (D) too much

( ) 5. I was only _____ to be given a chance to speak at the ceremony.
    (A) honored enough   (B) too honored
    (C) so much honor   (D) enough honor

解答：(A) (C) (A) (D) (B)

148

Part 10 | 感嘆句

1. 感嘆句基本上有兩種，包括以**What**和**How**開頭的句子。

❶ 感嘆句：How + adj. / adv. / 子句

……是多麼地/如此地……

❷ 感嘆句：What a/an + adj. + N

What a kind girl （she is）!

= How kind she is!

= How kind a girl she is!

= How kind the girl is!

她是多麼善良的女孩！

2. 感嘆句中what與how的分別

❶ How後面可以加上形容詞、副詞或子句，但是要搭配後面主要子句的句型。

❷ 以What開始的句子，後面一定要加上名詞，可以是單數名詞、複數名詞、不可數名詞等。如果是不可數或複數名詞，一律用What...!

• **How carefully they dealt with the suspicious bag!**

（→主要子句的動詞是一般動詞，所以前面要用副詞修飾）

他們是多麼小心地在處理這個可疑的袋子！

• **How efficiently they processed the application case!**

（→主要子句的動詞是一般動詞，所以前面要用副詞修飾）

他們處理這個申請案是多麼有效率呀！

• **How nervous he looked at the podium!**

（→主要子句的動詞是連綴動詞，所以前面要用形容詞修飾）

他在講台上看起來是多麼緊張啊！

- **How slim she has become!**

（→主要子句的動詞是連綴動詞，所以前面要用形容詞修飾）

她變得多麼苗條呀！

- **How she wishes she were capable enough to start her own company!**

（→主要子句中，沒有形容詞或副詞，所以直接接子句）

她多麼希望有能力可以自己開一家公司！

- **What charming voice she has!**

（→what後接複數名詞）

她所擁有的，是多麼迷人的嗓音呀！

- **What a strange stereotype you have for foreigners!**

（→what後接單數名詞）

你對外國人抱持的是多麼奇怪的刻板印象呀！

注意要點

要讚嘆的是單數可數名詞時，須要注意不定冠詞 a/an 的位置，來決定該以What或How開頭。以下的例句，請注意 a/an的位置，因為位置的不同，就要用不同的感嘆詞。

- **What a precious experience it is to interview a Nobel Prize winner!**

= How precious an experience it is to interview a Nobel Prize winner!

可以訪問諾貝爾獎得主是多麼珍貴的經驗呀！

Test 快來即時測驗自己的學習成果吧！

( ) 1. _____ TV program it is!
(A) How popular   (B) What a popular
(C) How a popular   (D) What popular

( ) 2. _____ they danced on the stage!
(A) What gracefully   (B) What graceful
(C) How graceful   (D) How gracefully

( ) 3. _____ they are to help the refugees!
(A) How kind   (B) How kindly
(C) What kindly   (D) What kind

( ) 4. _____ she introduced the new product of her company.
(A) What enthusiastically   (B) How enthusiastic
(C) How enthusiastically   (D) What an enthusiastic

( ) 5. _____ salesperson has become!
(A) What an experienced   (B) How experienced
(C) How an experienced   (D) What experienced

解答：(B) (C) (A) (D) (A)

Note

( ) 1. The exam was _____ I thought.
   (A) more difficult as
   (B) so much more difficult
   (C) not as difficult as
   (D) as much difficult

( ) 2. The smartphone is _____ as the laptop.
   (A) as a useful gadget
   (B) as useful a gadget
   (C) useful as a gadget
   (D) so much more useful gadget

( ) 3. We could offer assistance _____ you tell us exactly what you need.
   (A) as far as   (B) as much as   (C) as little as   (D) as long as

( ) 4. _____ you learn, _____ you realize you don't know.
   (A)The less; the more
   (B) The more; the more
   (C) The less; the less
   (D) The more; the less

( ) 5. Her apartment is _____ as mine.
   (A) twice larger
   (B) two times large
   (C) twice the size
   (D) twice as large

( ) 6. The bike is twice _____ the speed of a bus.
   (A) as slowly   (B) as slow as   (C) slower than   (D) so slow as

( ) 7. The sportscar is _____ as the moderate sedan.
   (A) three times more expansive   (B) three times the price
   (C) three times as expensive   (D) three times the price

( ) 8. Our performance is _____ satisfying to the manager. He thinks our work leaves a lot to be desired.
   (A) more than   (B) less than   (C) as much as   (D) as long as

( ) 9. He is _____ team player _____ a loner. He always works independently.
   (A) more; than   (B) as much; as   (C) less; than   (D) so much; as

( ) 10. What we could provide is _____ the data released by the authorities.

(A) less than (B) no more than

(C) not less than (D) not more than

( ) 11. The outbreak of the civil war was _____ thing we could predict.

(A) the most (B) the last (C) the more (D) the less

4

常
用
句
型

( ) 12. She is _____ skilled player on the school basketball team. No other player can play as well as she does.

(A) much more (B) the less (C) by far the most (D) far more

( ) 13. _____ was that our flight was canceled.

(A) Such terrible weather it (B) So terrible weather

(C) So terrible (D) Such terrible weather

( ) 14. We changed our itinerary _____ visit more scenic spots during the trip.

(A) so that (B) in order that (C) so as to (D) as long as

( ) 15. We could _____ his patience enough.

(A) hardly appreciate (B) admire

(C) never underestimate (D) not overemphasize

Chapter 5
假設語氣

1. 與現在事實相反的假設句型

★ 副詞子句

If S + V-p.t. / were / 過去式助動詞,

★ 主要子句

S + would / should / could / might + 動詞原型

2. 「與現在事實相反」if引導的子句，若是be動詞，一律用were，若是一般動詞，則用過去式，而主要子句動詞則為could/would/should/might＋VR。

3. if 子句的 **be** 動詞用 **were**，但口語中第一人稱和第三人稱單數用 **was**。

● If I had more money, I would choose a better car.
如果我有更多的錢，我就會選比較好的車。

● If he were at the ceremony, he would give a long speech.
如果他在典禮現場，他就會發表很長的感言。

● If I was/were hungry, I could have the desserts on the table.
如果我餓了，可以拿桌上的甜點來吃。

● If the solar panel were installed on the roof, it could convert the sunlight into electricity.
如果這個太陽能板能裝在屋頂，就可以將日光轉換成電力。

注意要點

if 子句中的 if 若省略，were 或助動詞必須提到句首形成倒裝。

- If James were intelligent enough, he could be recruited in the gifted class.

  = Were James intelligent enough, he could be recruited in the gifted class.

  如果詹姆士智商夠高，他就會去讀資優班。

- If my sister could bake cookies, she could make sponge fingers at home.

  = Could my sister bake cookies, she could make sponge fingers at home.

  如果我妹妹會烤餅乾的話，她就可以自己在家做手指餅乾了。

Test ——快來即時測驗自己的學習成果吧！

( ) 1. If I _____ the general manager, I would make a better decision.

    (A) am   (B) were   (C) could   (D) had

( ) 2. She would not attend the meeting if she _____ a choice.

    (A) have   (B) has   (C) had   (D) having

( ) 3. If Jackie _____ in the city, he could have access to more resource.

    (A) live   (B) living   (C) lives   (D) lived

( ) 4. If I _____ the address of the restaurant, I would go there right away.

    (A) know   (B) knows   (C) knew   (D) known

( ) 5. Jack would be very impressed if he _____ you sing the songs live today.

    (A) hear   (B) heard   (C) hears   (D) hearing

解答：(B) (C) (D) (C) (B)

Part 2 | 與過去事實相反的假設

1. 與「過去事實相反的假設」句型如下：

★ 副詞子句

If＋S＋had＋V-p.p.,

★ 假設語氣

S＋would/should/could/might＋have＋V-p.p.

2. 「與過去事實相反」，if引導的子句動詞須用had＋V-p.p.，而主要句動詞則為could/should/might＋have＋V-p.p.

- If you had registered for the conference, you could get the brochure for free.

  如果你有報名這個研討會，你就可以免費拿到這個冊子。

- If I had told her the truth, she would not have been so upset.

  如果我有告訴她實情，她就不會那麼生氣了。

- If I had the opportunity to interview for the position, I could display my portfolios.

  如果我有機會面試這個職位，我就可以展現我的作品集了。

延伸學習

1. 若if子句是「與過去事實相反」，而主要句是「與現在事實相反」，則全句意指「假如當時……，現在就……」。

2. 此種句型中，if子句常有then、before等表示過去時間的字詞，而主要句常有now、today等表示現在時間的字詞。

- If he had invested in the semiconductor industry, he would become a billionaire now.

  = He didn't invest in the semiconductor industry, and he is not a billionaire now.

  （→他之前沒有投資半導體產業，而他現在不是億萬富翁）

( ) 1. If he _____ his password, his account would not have been hacked.
   (A) had changed   (B) changes
   (C) changed   (D) should change

( ) 2. We _____ a new car, but we decided to stick with our old sedan.
   (A) have bought   (B) could buy
   (C) could have bought   (D) had bought

( ) 3. If Jerry _____ more careful, the fish would not have been burnt.
   (A) has been   (B) had been
   (C) would be   (D) were to be

( ) 4. We could not have reached Kevin if he _____ to another city.
   (A) had moved   (B) moves
   (C) were to move   (D) had moved

( ) 5. If the waste from the factory _____ properly treated, it would not have caused pollution in the region.
   (A) had been   (B) has been
   (C) were to be   (D) have to be

解答：(A) (C) (B) (D) (A)

159

Chapter5 假設語氣

Part 3 | 對未來事情的推測

 1. 與「未來預測之完全相反

1. 句型

★ 副詞子句

If＋S＋were to＋VR, (＝Were＋S＋to＋VR)

★ 主要子句

S＋would/should/could/might＋VR

2. 此句型強調未來事情發生的可能性近乎零，if子句不分人稱動詞一律用were to＋V，而主要子句動詞則為could/would/should/might＋VR，表示與未來事實相反。

• If I were to do space research, I would study the unknown substance on the surface of Mars.

= It is impossible for me to do space research, and I don't have the ability to study the unknown substances on the surface of Mars.

如果我能做太空研究，我就會去研究火星表面上的未知物質。

3. 此假設句用以表示和未來事實相反的情況。

• If his lost data were to be retrieved, he would become more stable emotionally.

如果他遺失的資料可以復原，他的情緒會比較穩定。

4. 此句型強調可預見的未來。

• If all the Greenland's ice sheet were to melt, some major cities around the world could be flooded.

如果格陵蘭的所有冰層都融化，有些主要城市將會被淹沒。

5. 此句型可用於提議，語氣比直接建議來得客氣。

● If the contract could be reviewed by our consultant beforehand, we could better know how it affects our right.

如果我們可以請顧問事先審閱這份合約，我們就可以更加了解它會如何影響我們的權益。

 2. 與「未來預測之萬一相反」

1. 句型

If＋S＋should＋VR , S＋will/shall/can/may＋VR
副詞子句.　　　　　　主要子句

= Should＋S＋to＋VR, S＋would/should/could/might＋VR
副詞子句　　　　　　　主要子句

2. 若表達對未來發生的可能性「強烈懷疑」，但不排除其發生的可能性，則if子句動詞一律用should＋VR，表示「萬一」，而主要句動詞則用would (will)/ could (can)/ should (shall)/ might (may)＋VR。

● If a super virus should spread across the globe, man could die out.

萬一有超級病毒傳播至全球，人類就有可能全部死亡。

● If he should call, take a message for me.

萬一他打電話來，請他留言給我。

3. 本句型用於未來假設，表示發生的可能性雖然不大但有可能，所以用if＋S＋should 表示「萬一」，主要子句的動詞也可用祈使句。

● If it should rain, take this umbrella with you.

萬一下雨的話，就把這把傘拿去用。

● You must remind me if I should miss any agenda item on the meeting.

=Please remind me if I should miss any agenda item on the meeting.

如果我在會議上漏掉任何議程，你得提醒我。

3. 描述「未來有可能改變的事實」

1. 句型

> If + S + 現在式V(代替未來), S + will / shall / can / may + VR.
> 副詞子句　　　　　　　　　主要子句

- If the temperature drops tomorrow, we will not go swimming.
  如果明天氣溫下降，我們就不會去游泳。

- If you don't stop procrastinating things, you will suffer a lot in the near future.
  如果你不改掉拖延的習慣，過不久你就會嚐到苦果。

2. 條件句常用if、when等連接詞，而且連接的子句中，雖然是未來可能發生的事，但動詞需用簡單現在式，而主要句的動詞，則用未來式。

- If water is boiled, it will become vapor.
  水被煮沸之後，就會變成水氣。

- If she is in a good mood, we will propose the project to her.
  假如她心情好的話，我們就會向她提議這案子。

3. if 所引導的子句，若表達未來可能發生，則稱為條件句，雖然中文說成「假使……；假設……」，但不是英文文法中的「假設語氣」句型。

- If she submits her article in time, it could be included in the journal.
  假如她及時繳交文章，它就會收錄在這本期刊中。

 4. 描述「條件與過去事實相反，結果與現在事實相反」的特殊句型

1. 句型

> If＋S＋had＋V-p.p.,　S＋would/should/could/might＋VR
> 副詞子句　　　　　　　　　主要子句
> （與過去相反）　　　　　　（與現在相反）

- If you hadn't participated in that luxurious trip, you wouldn't be short of money now.

  你如果沒去參加那場奢華旅行的話，你現在就不會這麼缺錢了。

- If I had got the college diploma, I could have more job opportunities now.

  如果我有大學文憑的話，我就會有更多的工作機會了。

Test ━━ 快來即時測驗自己的學習成果吧！

( ) 1. If the contract _____ revised, we would consider singing it.

  (A) could be (B) is (C) was (D) will have been

( ) 2. If the typhoon _____ the island, the flights will be canceled.

  (A) has hit (B) will hit (C) should hit (D) hits

( ) 3. If it _____ tomorrow, the field trip will be canceled.

  (A) rained (B) were to rain (C) rains (D) will have rained

( ) 4. If Michael _____ recruited in the national basketball team, he could play in the World Cup matches.

  (A) is (B) were to be (C) has been (D) will be

( ) 5. _____, we will have to change our schedule.

  (A) Should the meeting be postponed

  (B) If the meeting was postponed

  (C) If they postponed the meeting

  (D) If the meeting will be postponed

解答：(A) (D) (C) (B) (A)

Part 4 「若沒有……的話，就……」的表示法

1. 表達「現在若非……」的句型：

副詞子句	主要子句
But that/Only that＋S	
But for/Without＋N,＋現在式V,	S＋would/should/could/might＋動詞原型
If it were not for＋N,	
Were it not for＋N,	

2. 表達「過去若非……」的句型

★ 副詞子句

But that/Only that＋S
But for/Without＋N,＋過去式V,
If it had not been for＋N,
Had it not been for＋N,

★ 主要子句

S＋would/should/could/might＋have V-p.p.

3. if it were not for 表與現在事實相反的情況，而 **if it had not been for**則表示與過去事實相反，兩者皆可用 **but for**、**without** 來代替，之後接名詞片語。

4. 從**Without＋N**及**But for＋N**中無法判斷句子發生的時間，應從主要句的動詞型態中判斷是屬於「與現在事實相反」或是「與過去事實相反」。

5 if it were not for 和 if it had not been for 的 if 可省略，改成倒裝 were it not for 和 had it not been for。

- But for your support, I couldn't succeed.

  = But that you support me, I couldn't succeed.

  = If it were not for your support, I couldn't succeed.

  （→表現在情況，若非……）

  若不是你的支持，我不會成功。

- But for your support, I might have failed.

  = Without your support, I might have failed.

  = If it had not been for your support, I might have failed.

  = If you had not supported me, I might have failed.

  = But that you supported me, I might have failed.

  （→表過去情況，若非……）

  當時若不是你的支持，我很可能會失敗。

- Without your encouragement, I could not hang on.

  （→與現在事實相反）

  若非你的鼓勵，我現在也無法撐下去。

- Without your financial support, I could not have completed my education.

  （→與過去事實相反）

  若非有你的支持，我就無法完成我的學業。

注意要點

在美語口語中，if it were not for、if it had not been for 皆可用於與現在事實或過去事實相反，因此可聽到 if it were not for 之後接與過去事實相反的主要子句，反之亦然。

- If it were not for the message reminder, I might have forgotten to attend the meeting.

  要不是有簡訊提醒，我可能會忘記去參與會議。

1. if it were not for、if it had not been for 後接子句須先接名詞同位語 the fact。前者的 that 子句要用現在式，後者則用過去式。

- **If it were not for the fact that my parents are abroad, they would come to the banquet.**

  = But that my parents are abroad, they would come to the banquet.

  如果不是因為我父母在國外，他們會來參加宴會的。

2.but for可改成 but that＋S＋V 的形式，子句中的動詞不使用假設法，而是分別用現在式和過去式。

- **But that he gave me an advice, I could have made a terrible mistake.**

  要不是他當時給我忠告，我早就犯下大錯了。

3. 「若非……就……」的句型亦可用but that後接子句來表達，但子句用直說法，不用假設語氣。亦即表達「與現在事實相反」時，that子句的動詞用現在式；表達「與過去事實相反」時，則動詞用過去式。

- **But that you show up in time, the boss could go through the roof.**

  要不是你及時出現，老闆就會暴跳如雷了。

  （→與現在事實相反）

( ) 1. _____, I might have missed the deadline to apply for college admission.

    (A) Was it not for the reminder

    (B) If it had not been your message

    (C) If you do not remind me

    (D) Should you remind me

( ) 2. _____, I could give up on my studies.

    (A) But that he encourages me

    (B) If he had not encouraged me

    (C) If it has not been for his encouragement

    (D) Were he to encourage me

( ) 3. _____ familiar with the procedure, I could be the master of ceremony.

    (A) If I was   (B) If I will be   (C) If I were to be   (D) But that I am not

( ) 4. _____, the wounded girl could not be sent to the hospital in time.

    (A) But that we come to her rescue

    (B) If we were to come to her rescue

    (C) But that we came to her rescue

    (D) If were will come to her rescue

( ) 5. _____ in the seminar, we might not have learned so many professional terms.

    (A) If we had not participated

    (B) If we were to participate

    (C) But that we participate

    (D) If it were not for the participation

解答：(B) (A) (D) (A) (A)

ch **5** 假設語氣

1. 以 **as if/though** 表達「彷彿」的句型：

★ 副詞子句 (與過去事實相反)

　　S＋V＋as if/as though ,

　　S + were / V-p.t.

★ 主要子句 （與現在事實相反）

　　S＋ should/would/could/might have V-p.p.

2. 本句型的子句不是單純的「與現在事實相反」或「與過去事實相反」。

❶ as if假設句若與主要子句（不論現在式或過去式）同一時間發生，則子句動詞用過去式動詞。

❷ as if假設句比主要子句（不論現在式或過去式）更早發生，則子句動詞用had＋V-p.p.。

❸ as if後的子句有時會省略主詞與動詞，而成為片語。

- **He talks as if he were a linguistics expert.**

  （→副詞子句動詞were，與事實相反）

  他現在講話的樣子彷彿是個語言學專家。（他其實不是語言學專家）

- **He talked as if he were a linguistics expert.**

  （→副詞子句動詞were，與事實相反）

  他當時講話的樣子彷彿是個語言學專家似的。（他其實不是語言學專家）

- **The boys who shoplifted at the grocery store acted as if they had not done anything wrong.** （→與過去事實相反）

  在這間雜貨店偷東西的男孩表現得好像他們沒有做錯任何事情一樣。

- **She stood up as if to leave.** （→省略as if後的she was to）

  她站起來，彷彿要離開似的。

注意要點

as if 引導的子句也可描述「可能發生的事實」，此時動詞依照直說法規則即可，不需做變化。

● It looks as if the price of staple foods will rice in the following weeks.
看來糧食的價格在未來幾週會調漲。

Test ——快來即時測驗自己的學習成果吧！

( ) 1. It looks as if the typhoon _____ Taiwan next week.

(A) will hit   (B) had hit   (C) will have hit   (D) were to hit

( ) 2. Fiona ignored her ex-boyfriend as if they _____ each other.

(A) were not to know   (B) do not know

(C) did not know   (D) had not known

( ) 3. Linda spoke as if she _____ the research article, but she actually knew nothing about the study.

(A) could have read   (B) were to read

(C) will read   (D) had read

( ) 4. She walked around as if she _____ very busy with the house chores.

(A) had been   (B) was   (C) has been   (D) is

( ) 5. It looks as if the product _____ a lot of profit to the company in the following years.

(A) will bring   (B) brings

(C) had brought   (D) has brought

解答：(A) (B) (D) (C) (A)

Part 6 「但願」的表示法

1. 以If only等表達「但願」的句型：

❶ If only could/would＋VR（表未來但願）

❷ S＋wish/would rather that ＋ S ＋ were/V-p.t.（與現在事實相反）

❸ How I wish that had V-p.p.（與過去事實相反）

2. if only 用來表示與現在、過去、未來不同的希望，意思相當於 I wish（但願、要是……就好了）。

3. if only 用來表達和過去不同的希望，動詞用過去完成式；表達和現在不同的希望，子句動詞用過去式；表達和未來不符的希望時，動詞用**could/might/ would/should＋VR**

4. wish 表不可能發生的願望，若「與現在事實相反」，子句動詞用過去式；若與「過去事實相反」，子句動詞則用**had＋V-p.p**。此句型前常加上**how**，強調整個句子。本句型的I wish可替換成If only或Would that，用法及意思皆不變。

- Oh, no! There is a typo in my report. If only I had checked twice before submitting it.

  （→與過去事實相反）

  糟了，我的報告裡面有打錯字。如果我在繳交之前有再次檢查就好了。

- If only Mia had her employee ID with her, she could get into the office to collect her personal belongings.

  （→與現在事實相反）

  要是米亞有帶員工證就好了，她就可以去辦公室拿個人物品了。

- If only I would become more sophisticated, I could feel at ease during the business negotiation.

  （→對未來推測）

  但願我能變得更世故，就可以在商業談判場合中更加如魚得水。

- I wish I could joined the union, but I am not qualified yet.
  （→與現在事實相反）
  真希望我可以加入這個工會，但是我還不符合資格。

- I wish I had spent more time reviewing the lessons before the exam.
  （→與過去事實相反）
  我希望我考試之前有花多一點時間複習內容就好了。

- How I wish I hadn't said those offensive things to her.
  （→與過去事實相反）
  多麼希望我沒有對她說那些冒犯的話。

- I wish you had made a more comprehensive plan.
  = If only you had made a more comprehensive plan.
  = Would that you had made a more comprehensive plan.
  （→與過去事實相反）若是你有詳盡一些的計畫就好了。

延伸學習

1. wish 和 hope 中文意思類似，但wish可以表示與事實相反的假設或事實；而hope 表示可能實現的希望，後接直述句。但若要表達希望未來會發生的事，動詞需用hope，不是wish。

- The salesperson wishes he could improves his sales figures.
  這位銷售員希望可以改善自己的銷售成績。（→假設）

- She hopes she can be admitted to the medical school and become a pediatrician in the future.
  她希望她可以錄取醫學院，以後可以成為小兒科醫生。（→希望）

2. wish除了用在「與事實相反的」假設句外，亦可用來表示「祈求、祈願」。

- We wish you a merry Christmas and a happy New Year.
  祝你聖誕快樂，新年快樂。

- I wish you all the best.
  願你安好。

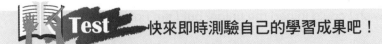

快來即時測驗自己的學習成果吧！

( ) 1. If only we _____ the map with us, we would not have to rely on Google Map.

(A) had   (B) have   (C) were to have   (D) will have

( ) 2. If only I _____ more organized, I could work more efficiently.

(A) could be   (B) had been   (C) was to be   (D) might be

( ) 3. I wish _____ enough brochures for all the participants, but not all of them get one last week.

(A) there will be   (B) there was

(C) there were   (D) there had been

( ) 4. I wish _____ me the truth. Then, I would have made a better decision.

(A) she will tell   (B) she tells

(C) she had told   (D) has told

( ) 5. If only _____ the baking class, but I have to prepare for the exam.

(A) I could attend   (B) I could have attended

(C) I will attend   (D) I have been attending

解答：(A) (C) (D) (A) (A)

Part **7** | 「是……的時候了」的表示法

1. 以**It's time...**表達「是……的時候了」的句型：

It's high / right / about / almost + time + for sb. to VR.

It's high / right / about / almost + time + that S + were / V-p.t.

2. 本句型「早該……了，但卻還沒」，故**It is time that**之後的子句動詞用過去式表示「與現在事實相反」。

3. 常在**time**之前加上**high**或**about**來修飾，加強語氣。

4. 同語意的句子，亦可用下列句型表達：

It is time (for＋sb.) to＋V... = It is time for＋N...

= It is time that＋S＋should＋V...

- It is time for us to hold an audition for the new movie.

=It is time for the audition for the new movie.

=It is time that we should hold an audition for the new movie.

該是我們為了新電影辦徵選的時候了。

- It is about time that the company should issue the year-end bonus.

=It is about time for the company to issue the year-end bonus.

=It is about time that the company issue the year-end bonus.

該是公司發年終獎金的時候了。

- It is high time for you to quit smoking.

=It is high time that you should quit smoking.

=It is high time that you quit smoking.

該是你要戒菸的時候了。

( ) 1. It's flu season again. It's high time that we _____ personal hygiene.

(A) emphasize (B) emphasized (C) will emphasize (D) emphasizing

( ) 2. It's about time that they _____ the required document.

(A) will submit (B) to submit (C) submitted (D) have to submit

( ) 3. It's time for you _____ a presentation about your product.

(A) to have made (B) making (C) to make (D) with making

( ) 4. It's high time _____ the vacation plan.

(A) for making   (B) to have made

(C) that we make   (D) that we should make

( ) 5. It's high time _____ the issue with our supervisor.

(A) for us to discuses (B) that we discuss

(C) should discuss   (D) to be discussed

解答：(B) (C) (C) (D) (A)

Note

Part 8 意志動詞及意志形容詞

1. 意志動詞列表

		that S2＋(should)＋VR
(1) 表「建議」	move propose advise recommend suggest	【要點】 (1) S1≠S2 (2) should 可以省略 (3) 意志動詞可以改成beV＋ 　　意志形容詞
(2) 表「堅持」	hold insist urge maintain	
(3) 表「要求」	ask request rule demand desire require provide stipulate	
(4) 表「命令」	order command direct	

2. 意志形容詞列表

It is	vital imperative proper advisable urgent mandatory necessary obligatory essential important	＋that＋S＋(should)＋VR (should通常省略)

- I insist that he (should) send the receipt in mail.

  = I insist on (/upon) his sending the receipt in mail.

  = I insist on (/upon) it that he (should) send the receipt in mail.

  我堅持他要用郵件寄送收據。

- Mary demanded that he modify the format of the report.

  瑪莉堅持要他修改報告的格式。

- The manager suggested that we postpone the promotion event.

  經理建議我們延後促銷的活動。

- It is urgent that a new production line (should) be added to the factory.

  在工廠中增加新的生產線是很迫切的事。

- It is necessary that the mistake (should) be amended right away.

  這件工作是必須立刻完成的。

- It is imperative that all of us (should) follow the regulations.

  我們必須遵守規定。

延伸學習

意志動詞也可改為名詞形式，並以作為強調的分裂句It beV...that 來表現。

- I suggest that he (should) alter his plan.

  = It is my suggestion that he (should) alter his plan.

  要他改變他的計劃，是我的建議。

- They insisted that they (should) be permitted into the municipal building.

  = It was their insistence that they (should) be permitted into the municipal building.

  他堅持他們應該獲准進入市政大樓。

- The customer made a request that the undercooked soup should be replaced with a new dish.

  客人要求沒煮熟的湯應該換成一道新的菜餚。

( ) 1. It is imperative that students _____ their admission ticket to get into the exam room.

(A) have　　(B) had　　(C) has　　(D) having

( ) 2. The boss demanded that all staff members _____ the morning session.

(A) attended　(B) will attend　(C) attend　(D) have attended

( ) 3. The soldier commended that all troops _____ to the camp.

(A) retreated　　　　　　(B) retreat
(C) have retreated　　　　(D) will retreat

( ) 4. It is mandatory that plastic beverage straws _____ replaced with paper ones.

(A) should be　　　　　　(B) will be
(C) are　　　　　　　　　(D) have been

( ) 5. The medical professional recommended that everyone _____ facial masks when they go to the hospital.

(A) should wear　　　　　(B) can wear
(C) wear　　　　　　　　(D) wears

解答：(A) (C) (B) (A) (C)

1. If 的同義詞

★ 片語

　　Given that

　　In case that

　　In the event that

　　On condition that

★ 分詞片語

　　Suppose / Supposing

　　Provide / Providing

　　Assumed / Assuming

　　Granted / Granting

2. provided (that)、providing (that) 用來引導條件子句，與 if/on condition that as/so long as 意思相同。

3. given 之後可接名詞或子句，可用於引導條件子句或假設句。

- **Provided that he quits using profane language, he could be a great teacher.**

  假如他不再說髒話的話，他會是一位很好的老師。

- **Supposing she brings your lost dog back home, how will you reward her?**

  假如她把你走丟的狗送回家，你會怎麼答謝她呢？

- **Given the opportunity, I will be a volunteer of a charity organization.**

  = If I am given the opportunity, I will be a volunteer of a charity organization.

  如果有機會，我就會去慈善機構做義工。

- Given enough time, I would make some modifications in my manuscript.

= If I were given more time, I would make some modifications in my manuscript.

要是我有更多時間的話,我就會對手稿做一些修改。

Test ——快來即時測驗自己的學習成果吧!

( ) 1. Supposing she _____ to the class today, I could return the notebook to her.

(A) comes   (B) come   (C) came   (D) have come

( ) 2. Given that more people _____ in the campaign, the work could be completed more efficiently.

(A) have participated   (B) should participate

(C) participate   (D) participating

( ) 3. Provided that we _____ the game, we could go through the next round.

(A) winning   (B) have won   (C) won   (D) win

( ) 4. On condition that we _____ the reference book at hand, we could check the professional terms right away.

(A) having   (B) to have   (C) had   (D) have

( ) 5. In case that the souvenir store is closed today, we _____ tomorrow.

(A) would have come   (B) have to come again

(C) should have come   (D) will have come

解答:(A) (C) (D) (D) (B)

Part 10 | 表達推測的助動詞

1. 「過去式語氣助動詞＋**have＋V-p.p.**」亦可表示「過去該……，但是卻未如此」的意思，要根據上下文判定其義。句型為：

❶ ought to / could / should / might / would ＋ have ＋ V-p.p.
「過去該……，但是卻未如此」

❷ needn't＋have＋V-p.p.　「過去不必……，但是卻如此」

❸ must＋have＋V-p.p.　　「過去一定……」，表對過去的猜測

2. would/could/should＋have＋V-p.p.

表示「與過事實相反」，事情「本將／本可／本該做而沒有做」

- The show last night was fantastic. You should have come with us.
  昨晚的表演精彩極了。你應該跟我們一起去看的。

- Gina looked exhausted this morning. She might have burnt the midnight oil last night.
  吉娜今天早上看起來很累。她昨晚應該是熬夜了。

- Based on the information we have received, the illegal drug could have been smuggled to the foreign country.
  根據我們得到的消息，非法藥品應該是被走私到國外了。

延伸學習

1. must have＋V-p.p.表「對過去的強烈推測」，不是「本必須做而沒有做」。

否定句用can't have＋V-p.p.。

2. 「對現在的強烈推測」，則用must＋V，否定句用can't＋V。

- She has puffy eyes today. She must have cried yesterday.
  她眼睛腫腫的。她一定是昨天哭過。（→對過去的推測）

- James hasn't come back from the United States. You can't have seen him in class this morning.
  詹姆士還沒有從美國回來。你們今天早上上課時不可能看到他。
  （→對過去的推測）

- The ground is wet. I guess it might have rained last night.
  地板是濕的。我猜昨晚應該下過雨。

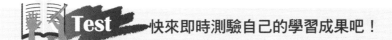

Test ──快來即時測驗自己的學習成果吧！

( ) 1. She _____ your diary. Otherwise, she couldn't have learned about the secret.
 (A) has read   (B) were to read
 (C) has been reading   (D) must have read

( ) 2. According to the report, the gangster _____ in the gunfight.
 (A) were killed   (B) has been killed
 (C) might have been killed (D) were to be killed

( ) 3. Kevin _____ the goods. The supplier hasn't delivered them yet.
 (A) could not have received (B) might have received
 (C) were to receive   (D) will have received

( ) 4. You _____ to the party. The host prepared a surprise for you, but you weren't there.
 (A) were to come   (B) should have come
 (C) will have come   (D) can come

( ) 5. I couldn't reach her through cellphone. She _____ another country.
 (A) might have gone to (B) has been to
 (C) went to   (D) should go to

解答：(D) (C) (A) (B) (A)

Part 11 表示「寧願……而不願……」的動詞

1. 以**would rather**等字表示「寧願……而不願……」的句型如下：

❶ S＋would rather VR than VR　S＋would sooner VR than VR
　S＋would VR rather than VR

❷ S＋prefer to VR rather than VR
　S＋prefer to VR instead of V-ing
　S＋prefer V-ing/N to V-ing/N

2. would rather...than...的注意要點如下：

❶ would rather...than 中的 than 為連接詞，連接對等的結構，動詞須用原形，若前後動詞相同時，可省略後面的動詞。

❷ 本句型would rather為固定用法，用法等於would sooner，後接原形動詞。

❸ 本句型也可將rather置於than之前，成為would...rather than...。

3. would rather...than...也可用 prefer to...rather than...代替。

❶ prefer to...rather than...中 rather than 為連接詞，前後須連接VR。

❷ rather than的意思等於instead of，所以prefer to V1 rather than V2的句型可寫成prefer to VR rather than VR。但要留意的是，instead of須加V-ing。而prefer...to...的句型意為「喜歡……勝過……」，不同的是prefer及to之後接須接名詞或動名詞。

4. instead of 的注意要點如下：

❶ instead 作副詞用，可置於句首或句尾，置於句首要用逗號與句子分開。

❷ instead of 與rather than為介詞片語，之後接名詞或動名詞，表示「不……而是……；代替……」的意思，與 rather than 意思相同。rather than 作連接詞用時，前後詞語的詞性必須對等。

❸ 這裡的rather than連接不定詞片語時，後面的不定詞 to 常會省略。

- He would rather starve than receive help from his enemy.
  = He would starve rather than receive help from his enemy.
  = He prefers to starve rather than receive help from his enemy.
  = He prefers to starve instead of receiving help from his enemy.
  他寧可餓死，也不願接受敵人的幫助。

- James would rather quit than reconcile to the unreasonable rules.
  = James prefers to quit rather than reconcile to the unreasonable rules.
  = James prefers quitting to reconciling to the unreasonable rules.
  = James prefers to quit instead of reconciling to the unreasonable rules.
  詹姆士寧願辭職也不願對不合理的規定妥協。

- Tim would rather deal with the chores himself than hiring an assistant.
  提姆寧可自己做雜事也不要雇用一個助理。

- I prefer Japanese cuisines to Western ones.
  我喜歡日本菜勝過西式菜餚。

- What they need is advice instead of flattery.
  他們需要的是建議而非奉承。

- He didn't accept our suggestion but adopted that impracticable plan instead.
  他沒有接受我們的建議，反而採用了不實際的計畫。

- Rather than seeking sympathy from your friends, you should put yourself together and find a good solution.
  你應該振作起來，找出解決方案，而不是向朋友討拍。

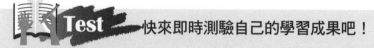

( ) 1. Fiona _____ in the contest, but she didn't get any prize in the end.

(A) had won　(B) will have won　(C) could have won　(D) might win

( ) 2. Beth _____ the poor family, but she did a lot for them.

(A) needn't have helped　　　(B) could not help

(C) will have helped　　　　(D) has been heaping

( ) 3. Peter _____ the exam. He looks exhilarated.

(A) need to pass　　　　　(B) will have passed

(C) must have passed　　　(D) could have passed

( ) 4. She _____ the package. I just saw it on the table.

(A) has sent　　　　　　　(B) might have sent

(C) shouldn't have sent　　(D) can't have sent

( ) 5. There are some footprints on the floor. Someone _____ into the house.

(A) will be breaking　　　　(B) must have broken

(C) might have been broke　(D) had broken

解答：(C) (A) (C) (D) (B)

Note

(   ) 1. There are some typo in the report. You _____ more careful.
    (A) should have been   (B) needn't have been
    (C) could have been   (D) will have been

(   ) 2. If she _____ more time, she would revise the proposal.
    (A) had   (B) has   (C) will have   (D) had had

(   ) 3. What would you do if you _____ homeless people walk toward you on the street.
    (A) saw   (B) see   (C) have seen   (D) had seen

(   ) 4. The kids could have some snacks if they _____ the task within 3 minutes.
    (A) have finished (B) had finished (C) finish   (D) will finish

(   ) 5. If Jenny _____, she wouldn't have lost such a large amount of money.
    (A) invests in the stock market   (B) sold her apartment a month ago
    (C) had not trusted that con artist   (D) can purchase the sportscar

(   ) 6. She could have got a raise if she _____ better last year.
    (A) performed   (B) has performed
    (C) had performed   (D) could have performed

(   ) 7. If I _____ the file before the computer crashed, I wouldn't have to start all over again.
    (A) haven't saved (B) had saved (C) have saved (D) hadn't saved

(   ) 8. If we _____ an expert, we could know better about this subject.
    (A) might have consulted   (B) could consult
    (C) needn't consult   (D) will consult

( ) 9. Please remind me if I _____ any detail.
(A) will miss   (B) may miss   (C) have missed (D) should miss

( ) 10. If the new technology _____ in the factory, the productivity could be much higher.
(A) might be used   (B) will be used (C) is used   (D) could be used

( ) 11. Cover the machine if it _____ so that there wouldn't be rust on the surface of the machine.
(A) had rained   (B) should rain   (C) could rain   (D) has rained

( ) 12. _____, he would quit the idea of starting his own business.
(A) If he has failed again   (B) Should he fail again
(C) If he had failed again   (D) Had he failed again

( ) 13. If he _____ the rumor on the Internet, he will be fined for violating the new law.
(A) spreads   (B) spread   (C) have spread   (D) would spread

( ) 14. _____ Bill made a large donation to the charity organization, many poor kids could not have had normal education.
(A) But that   (B) Should   (C) Had   (D) Had it not been

( ) 15. The con artist acted as if he _____ the oil company in the Middle East.
(A) had   (B) has   (C) has had   (D) will have

ch **5**
假設語氣

解答 : 1. (A) 2. (A) 3. (A) 4. (C) 5. (C) 6. (C) 7. (D) 8. (B) 9. (D) 10. (D) 11. (B) 12. (B) 13. (A) 14. (A) 15. (A)

Chapter 6
倒裝句型

Part 1 | 否定副詞的倒裝句型

1. 否定副詞（或具否定意義的片語）放句首時，其後子句需用倒裝句。

❶ 若原子句是主詞加be動詞時，直接把主詞與be動詞對調成倒裝。

　句型：否定副詞＋beV＋S

❷ 若原子句是主詞加一般動詞時，則在主詞前面加上助動詞，形成倒裝。**句型：**否定副詞＋助V＋S＋VR

❸ 請注意，若原子句是完成式，原是S＋have/has/had＋V-p.p.，其倒裝句型：否定副詞＋have/has/had＋S＋V-p.p.

2. 常用的否定副詞列表

　　❶ hardly/barely/rarely/scarcely/seldom 幾乎不

　　❷ few（可數）/little（不可數）幾乎沒有

　　❸ no sooner/no more/no longer 不再

　　❹ never(again) 再也不；never(before)=not for a moment 從來沒有

　　❺ not until 不⋯⋯直到

　　❻ without effect/without avail/in vain 沒有用

　　❼ not a/not an/not any 沒有任何一個

　　❽ not at all/not in the least 一點也不

　　❾ in no way/on no account/in no case/on no condition/by no means/under no circumstances/to no purpose 絕不

- **It is seldom wise to trust a stranger.**
  = Seldom is it wise to trust a stranger.

  （→保留be動詞**is**）相信陌生人不是一個明智之舉。

- She rarely keeps her word.

  = Rarely does she keep her word.

  （→動詞為第三人稱現在式，用助動詞does）

  她很少信守諾言。

- I have never tried scuba diving in my whole life.

  = In my whole life I have never tried scuba diving.

  = Never in my whole life have I tried scuba diving.

  （→動詞為第一人稱完成式，用完成式have）

  我從來沒嘗試過水肺潛水。

- Hardly was he （→原句：He was hardly）aware that the pickpocket took away his wallet.

  當扒手拿走他的皮夾時，他沒有察覺。

- **Never have smartphones been made before** （→原句： Smartphones have never been made before）**so efficient, stylish, and well-developed as those of today.**

  以前的智慧型手機從來沒有像今天的這麼有效率、有型、又進步。

　　表達「絕對不允許」或「絕對不能」的否定詞，置於句首時，後面引導的句子需倒裝，倒裝的結構和疑問句的結構一樣；即「助V＋S＋V...」或「BeV＋S...」，完成式則用「has/have/had＋S＋V-p.p.」。和by no means（絕不）同義的否定詞尚有：in no way/on no account/in no case/on no condition/under no circumstances/to no purpose。

- **By no means did we enter the manager's office without his permission.**

  沒有經理的允許，我們絕不能進去他的辦公室。

- **On no account did Mandy allow her son to spend a whole evening at the electric arcade.**

  曼蒂絕不允許她兒子花一整個晚上在電動遊樂場。

( ) 1._____satisfied with our performance.

(A) Never did she   (B) Never will she

(C) Never was she   (D) Never has she

( ) 2. _____ show up in the seminars throughout the academic year.

(A) Seldom did he   (B) Never has he

(C) Seldom is he   (D) Never was he

( ) 3. _____ made mistakes in her report over the last two years.

(A) Never did she   (B) Never has she

(C) Seldom was he   (D) Never was he

( ) 4. _____ discouraged by the failure. He just kept trying.

(A) Never was he   (B) Seldom would he

(C) Never did he   (D) Hardly was he

( ) 5. On no condition _____ the house with such a small budget.

(A) could we renovate   (B) are we renovating

(C) have renovated   (D) could be renovated

解答：(C) (A) (B) (A) (A)

Note

Part 2 | only的倒裝句型

only的意思為「只有」，若接副詞子句或副詞片語，其後之主要子句需倒裝。only之後引導的副詞子句不需倒裝。句型：

Only + 介系詞片語 / 副詞子句/ 副詞 + be + S

Only + 介系詞片語 / 副詞子句/ 副詞＋助 V + S + VR

- **Only in their hometown can they feel comfortable.**
（→only＋介詞片語）

  只有在他們自己的家鄉才會覺得自在。

- **Only when the investors can predict a bull market will they buy stocks.**（→only＋副詞子句）

  只有當投資者預測股市將上漲的時候，他們才會買股票。

- **You can reach your full potential only by working hard.**
  Only by working hard can you reach your full potential.
（→only＋介詞片語）唯有透過努力工作，你才能發揮全部的潛力。

- **We can improve our work efficiency only by managing our time well.**
  Only by managing our time well can we improve our work efficiency.（→only＋介詞片語）

  唯有好好地安排時間才能增加我們的工作效率。

注意要點

only置句首時，後面不是接副詞子句或副詞片語，則主要子句不需倒裝。

- **Only you can help me.**
  只有你能幫助我。

「Only＋副詞子句＋助動詞＋S＋V...」句型可替換為
「not...until...」。

• I had a feast only after the college entrance exam was over.
  = Only after the college entrance exam was over did I have a feast.
  = Not until the college entrance exam was over did I have a feast.
  我在大學入學考試結束之後才去享用大餐。

Test 快來即時測驗自己的學習成果吧！

( ) 1._____ the typhoon land warming was lifted could the technician start to fix the damaged system.

(A) Not until   (B) Never   (C) Hardly   (D) Only

( ) 2. _____ can we know more about the consumers' needs.

(A) Never could conducting a survey   (B) Without conducting a survey

(C) Only by conducting a survey   (D) Hardly with a survey

( ) 3. Not until she showed us the document _____ about the confidential data.

(A) that we know   (B) have we known

(C) did we learn   (D) will we see

( ) 4. _____ will the shoppers purchase the product.

(A) Only if there is a discount   (B) Hardly when there is a discount

(C) Were there to be a discount   (D) Not until there was a discount

( ) 5. Only by calling the hotel directly _____ whether there is a vacant room on the designated date.

(A) will be able to know   (B) were we to know

(C) have we known   (D) can you know

解答：(D) (A) (C) (C) (A) (D)

194

Part **3** | No sooner 的 倒裝句型

1. no sooner為否定詞，置於句首時其後引導的句子需用倒裝句。整個句型表示「一……就……」。句型為：

No sooner had S＋V-p.p. than S＋V-p.t.

2. 連接詞than所引導的子句不需倒裝，子句裡的動詞用過去簡單式。

3. 此句型描述兩動作發生的先後次序，主要子句的動作先發生，用過去完成式(had＋V-p.p.)，than引導的子句動作後發生，用過去簡單式(V-p.t.)。

4. 同義句型列表

❶ The moment/minute/instant S＋V-p.t...., S＋V-p.t....

❷ Once/Directly/Instantly/Immediately S＋V-p.t...., S＋V-p.t....

❸ On/Upon＋V-ing, S＋V-p.t.

❹ As soon as S＋V-p.t., S＋V-p.t.

= S＋had no sooner＋V-p.p. than S＋V-p.t.

= No sooner had S＋V-p.p. than S＋V-p.t.

❺ S＋had hardly/scarcely＋V-p.p. when/before S＋V-p.t.

= Hardly/Scarcely had＋S＋V-p.p. when/before S＋V-p.t.

● The moment she saw the diamond ring, she had a smile on her face.

= Directly she saw the diamond ring, she had a smile on her face.

= On/Upon seeing the diamond ring, she had a smile on her face.

= As soon as she saw the diamond ring, she had a smile on her face.

= No sooner had she seen the diamond ring than she had a smile on her face.

= She had hardly seen the diamond ring before she had a smile on her face.

= Hardly had she seen the diamond ring before she had a smile on her face.

她一看到鑽戒，臉上就出現笑容。

- As soon as the government announced the policy, the labor union launched strikes.

= The government had no sooner announced the policy than the labor union launched strikes.

= No sooner had the government announced the policy than the labor union launched strikes.

政府一宣布新政策，勞工團體就發起罷工。

- The moment the newspaper secured the major scoop, it broke the scandal to the world.

= On securing the major scoop, the newspaper broke the scandal to the world.

報社一搶到了重要的獨家新聞，就把這件醜聞公諸於世。

- I had scarcely finished the test questions when the bell ring.

= Scarcely had I finished the test questions when the bell ring.

= I heard the bell ring as soon as I finished the test questions.

我才剛做完考題就聽到鈴聲響了。

Note

( ) 1. _____ at the bus stop when the bus left.

(A) Hardly had she arrived

(B) She hardly arrives

(C) Hardly does she arrive

(D) Hardly will she arrive

( ) 2. _____ was the road closed.

(A) The car accident hardly happened

(B) Hardly will the car accident happen

(C) Hardly could the car accident happen

(D) Hardly had the car accident happened

( ) 3. _____ me than I saw him across the street.

(A) Hardly had he called

(B) Hardly does he call

(C) No sooner had he called

(D) Not until he calls

( ) 4. _____ did they show up at the meeting.

(A) No sooner had we went through the agendas

(B) Not until we went through the agendas

(C) Hardly did we go through the agendas

(D) As soon as we went through the agendas

( ) 5. _____ the bad news before she passed out.

(A) She had hardly heard

(B) Hardly did she hear

(C) No sooner had she hear

(D) Scarcely had she heard

解答：(A) (D) (C) (B) (A)

Part 4 | Not until 的 倒裝句型

1.此句型「S＋助動詞＋not＋V...＋until＋子句／時間副詞」，為「直到……才……」的加強語氣句型。因為否定字not至句首，後之主要子句需倒裝，形成「Not until＋子句／時間副詞＋助動詞＋S＋V...」的句型。

2.until以及not...until的差別

❶ till=until：（表示動作、狀態的持續）一直……為止

❷ not...until：直到……才……

- She delayed working on the report until the day before the deadline.

  = She did not work on the report until the day before the deadline.

  = Not until the day before the deadline did she work on the report.

  她直到期限前一天才做報告。

- He lived in Tainan until he was transferred to the headquarter in Taipei.

  = He did not move from Tainan to Taipei until he was transferred to the headquarter in Taipei.

  = Not until he was transferred to headquarter in Taipei did he move from Tainan to Taipei.

  他直到調職到台北的總部之前都住在台南。

- Not until the party was over did they show up.

  直到派對結束他們才出現。

- Not until his mother got sick did he realized that he spent too little time accompanying her.

  直到母親生病時，他才發現自己花太少時間陪她了。

「Not until＋子句／時間副詞＋助動詞＋S＋V...」也可以分裂句「It＋be動詞＋not until＋子句／時間副詞＋that＋S＋V...」的形式呈現，強調用法。此句型裡連接詞that引導的子句不須倒裝，until引導的子句為副詞子句，也不須倒裝。而主要子句倒裝的結構和疑問句的結構一樣。

- He did not complete his college education until he was 27.

  = Not until he was 27 did he complete his college education.

  = It was not until he was 27 that he completed his college education.

  他直到27歲才完成大學教育。

- I don't understand how much effort she had made until I see her portfolio.

  = Not until I see her portfolio do I understand how much effort she had made.

  = It is not until I see her portfolio that I understand how much effort she had made.

  直到我看到她的作品集，才瞭解她付出多少努力。

( ) 1._____ did she change her mind.
   (A) Not until we talked to her   (B) It was not until we talked to her
   (C) Not until we talk   (D) We didn't talk to her

( ) 2. Not until the computer was fixed _____ our work.
   (A) that we resumed   (B) could we resume
   (C) had we resumed   (D) will we resume

( ) 3. It was not until 8:00 this morning _____ to attend the meeting.
   (A) that we were informed   (B) did we inform
   (C) will we inform   (D) that we informed

( ) 4. Not until he got home _____ that he left his glasses at the office.
   (A) did he realize   (B) that he realized
   (C) was he realized   (D) does he realize

( ) 5. It was not until it rained _____.
   (A) will we head home
   (B) did we cancel the trip
   (C) had we changed the route
   (D) that the fire was distinguished

解答：(A) (B) (A) (A) (D)

200

Part 5 | As ……, so ……的句型

此句型用來表示「A之於B猶如C之於D」。有下列同義句型：

A is to B as/what C is to D

= As C is to D, so is A to B

= As C is to D, so A is to B

= What C is to D, so A is to B

= What C is to D, (that) A is to B

- Music is to the mind as / what oxygen is to the body.

  = As oxygen is to the body, so is music is to the mind.

  = What oxygen is to the body, music is to the mind.

  音樂之於心靈猶如空氣之於身體。

- The rumor is to a society as the poison to the human body.

  = The rumor is to a society what the poison is to the human body.

  = As the poison is to the human body, so is the rumor to the society.

  = As the poison is to the human body, so the rumor is to the society.

  = What poison is to the human body, the rumor is to the society.

  謠言之於社會猶如毒藥之於人體。

 快來即時測驗自己的學習成果吧！

(　) 1. _____, the skin is to human body.

    (A) The bark is to the tree

    (B) What the bark is to the tree

    (C) As the bark is to the tree

    (D) The bark is to the tree

(　) 2. As a pen is to a writer, _____.

    (A) so is a knife to a chef

    (B) the knife is to a chef

    (C) what a knife is to a chef

    (D) so the knife is to a chef

(　) 3. The crest is to a family _____.

    (A) , the flag is to a nation

    (B) , so the flag is to a nation

    (C) , so is the flag to a nation

    (D) as the flag is to a nation

(　) 4. _____, reading is to human mind.

    (A) What exercise is to the body

    (B) As exercise is to the body

    (C) Exercise is to the body

    (D) Exercise is to the body

(　) 5. What sonar is to a dolphin, _____.

    (A) as the map to a hiker

    (B) so is the map to a hiker

    (C) the map is to a hiker

    (D) so the map is to a hiker

解答：(B) (A) (D) (A) (C)

202

Part **6** | not only 的 倒裝句型

1.「**not only A but (also) B**」的句型表示「不只……還有……」，**A 和B 須連接**性質相同的字詞。

2. **not**為否定字詞，置於句首時，後面引導的子句倒裝。**but**之後的動詞片語或子句皆不須倒裝，但時態須與前面動詞一致。

3. 句型中**only**可替換為**just**或**merely**。

- She not only prepared meals for the elderly people, but also accompanied them.

  = Not only did she prepare meals for the elderly people, but also accompanied them.

  她不僅為長者準備餐點，還陪伴他們。

- Jo not only dances well, but also makes delicious desserts.

  = Not only does Jo dance well, but she also makes delicious desserts.

  喬不僅跳舞跳得許好，也會做好吃的點心。

- Rose not only designed the house, but she also built it with her own hands.

  = Not only did Rose design the house, but she also built it with her own hands.

  蘿絲不僅設計了這間房子，還親手建造了它。

連接句子時，also 必須置於動詞之前、be 動詞之後。

- **The workers not only work efficiently, but they also do things meticulously.**
  工人們不只有效率地工作，也細心地做事。

- **Kevin is not only my supervisor, but also my mentor.**
  = **Not only is Kevin my supervisor, but he is also my mentor.**
  凱文不僅是我的主管，也是我的導師。

❶ 在同一個子句中，not only A but (also) B 的語意重點在B，故動詞以主詞B為主。句型為：Not only A but (also) B＋V（視B決定）

- **Not only Kate but also her parents hit the jackpot.**
  不只凱特，連她的父母都贏得大獎。

- **Not only he alone but we are also the advocators of environmental protection.**
  不只有他一人，還有我們，都是環保的提倡者。

❷ not only A but(also)B也等同於A as well as B（A以及B），但A as well as B的語意重點在A，故動詞以主詞A為主。句型：

A as well as B＋V（視A決定）

❸ 在句意上，as well as=along with=together with。

- **My father as well as I is trying to repair the car.**
  我父親和我都在嘗試要修理這台車。

- **My cousin as well as I takes my uncle as a role model.**
  我表弟和我都以我的叔叔為榜樣。

- **Linda as well as her sisters can act well, so they would all go to the audition for the movie.**
  琳達和她的姊姊演戲都演得很好，所以他們會去參加電影的試鏡。

( ) 1. Nancy as well as you _____ hard. I believe you will both get high scores in the test.

(A) studies   (B) study   (C) are studying   (D) have studied

( ) 2. David as well as I_____ the project seriously.

(A) take   (B) are taking   (C) have taken   (D) takes

ch
6
倒裝句型

( ) 3. _____, but she is also my bosom friend.

(A) Mandy was not only my classmate

(B) Not only is Mandy my sister

(C) Mandy is not only a colleague

(D) Not only was Mandy my partner

( ) 4. The boy is not only confident in himself, _____ considerate to others.

(A) he was as well

(B) and he was also

(C) but he is also

(D) but also is he

( ) 5. _____, but he is also frustrated about this matter.

(A) Not only was he upset

(B) He not only is upset

(C) Not only is he upset

(D) He is not only upset

解答：(A) (D) (D) (B) (C)

Chapter6 倒裝句型

Part 7 | So, Neither, Not 作為附和的倒裝句型

 1. so的倒裝句型

1. so 表示贊同的附和句，就是「也」的意思。

A: I enjoy playing water sports.
我喜歡水上運動。

B: I do, too./So do I.
我也喜歡。

2.neither和nor的用法一樣，都是表否定的附和句，是「也不」的意思。

● A: I am not playing an online game.
我沒有在玩線上遊戲。

B: I am not, either. 或 Neither/Nor am I.
我也沒有。

3. so/neither（也／也不……）在此為副詞，句子之間需用連接詞 **and**或分號（;）或句點隔開，之後的句子須倒裝，助動詞／**be**動詞用肯定。句型為：

> 肯定句,and so＋助動詞／be動詞＋S（皆為也……）
>
> =肯定句,and＋S＋助動詞／be動詞, too.

● A: I like romantic comedies.
   B: I like romantic comedies, too.
   = I do, too.
   = So do I.

● You are an engineer, and Diana is, too. → and so is Diana.
你是工程師，黛安娜也是。

- Alice can play electric guitar, and Nancy can, too.
  → and so can Nancy.
  艾莉絲會彈電吉他，南西也是。

- She was exhausted, and so were her colleagues.
  她累壞了，她的同事也是。

- I enjoy skiing; so does my husband.
  我喜歡滑雪，我先生也喜歡。

2. neither的倒裝句型

1. neither用來表達「附和」之意時，句型和so相同。句型為：否定句，and neither＋助動詞／be動詞＋S（……也不……）否定句，and＋S＋助動詞/be動詞＋not, either.

2.「neither A nor B」的句型則是表達「既不……也不……」，連接兩個子句，A和B須詞性相同。若主詞相同時，則nor引導的子句中，「助動詞＋主詞」可以省略。neither或nor為否定字詞，置於句首時，後面引導的句子須倒裝。

A: I don't like the anchor who is sarcastic while reporting the news.
B:I don't like the anchor who is sarcastic while reporting the news, either.
= I don't, either. = Neither do I.
A：我不喜歡那個在播報新聞時很諷刺的主播。
B：我也是（我也不喜歡）。

- He won't participate in the contest, and I won't, either.
  → and neither will I. → and nor will I.
  他不會參加比賽，我也不會。

- He is not in the Board of Directors; neither am I.
  他不是董事會的成員，我也不是。

- My brother doesn't like entertaining the clients, nor do I.
  我弟弟不喜歡和客戶應酬，我也是。

- I like neither squid nor shrimp.
  我既不喜歡魷魚，也不喜歡蝦子。

- Neither did Kevin admit his mistakes nor want to apologize.
  凱文既不想要承認他的錯誤，也不想要道歉。

neither A nor B（既不……也不……）或其類似句型either A or B（不是……就是……）的句型中，A和B須對等，亦即連接性質相同的字詞，動詞以最靠近的主詞B為主。句型為：

❶ Neither A nor B＋V （視B決定）...

❷ Either A or B＋V （視B決定）...

- **Neither she nor I has negative comments on this movie.**
  她和我對這部電影都沒有負評。

- **Either your sister or you have to sign the surgery agreement to save your mother.**
  你姊姊或是你需要簽手術同意書來救你的母親。

雖然「either A or B」類似句型「neither A nor B」，但either並非否定字詞，置於句首時，後面引導的子句不須用倒裝句，or之後的子句也不須倒裝。

- **The playboy from a rich family either fool around or bully the servants.**
  這個有錢人家的紈褲子弟不是無所事事就是欺負僕人。

- **Either we change the terms of the contract, or we lose the client.** 我們不是更改條合約條文，就是失去客戶。

( ) 1. _____ fix the machine nor inform the maintenance staff.
(A) He has neither   (B) Neither did he
(C) He did not   (D) Either did he

( ) 2. Mandy didn't receive the reminder email; _____.
(A) so do I   (B) either do I
(C) neither did I   (D) neither do I

( ) 3. _____he come to the meeting nor called in sick this morning.
(A) Neither did   (B) Either will
(C) Neither that   (D) Either

( ) 4. _____ she comes to our office, or we have an online interview with her.
(A) Neither   (B) Either
(C) Not only   (D) Not until

( ) 5. Mandy won't attend the year-end party, _____.
(A) neither do I   (B) and neither do I
(C) neither will I   (D) and neither will I

解答：(B) (C) (A) (B) (D)

Note
- -
- -
- -
- -
- -
- -

Part 8 | So...that.../ Such...that...的倒裝句型

1. so...that及such...that的句型，原本結構為：

S＋beV＋so＋adj.＋that＋S＋V...

S＋beV＋such＋名詞＋that＋S＋V...

動詞為be動詞，so＋adj. 及such＋名詞為主詞補語，若為了強調此補語而將補語放句首，其後引導的子句則須用倒裝結構。

2. 倒裝的是主要句，連接詞that所引導的子句，則不須用倒裝形式。

- Jerry is so creative that he could invent many different cuisines.

  = So creative is Jerry that he could invent many different cuisines.

  = Such is Jerry's creativity that he could invent many different cuisines.

  （→補語為adj. creative 時，搭配副詞so；補語為N creativity 時，搭配形容詞such）

  傑瑞是那麼創意，可以發明不同的菜餚。

- He danced so well that he won the champion in the contest.

  = So well did he dance that he won the champion in the contest.

  （→補語為adv.well，搭配副詞so）

  他跳舞跳得那麼好，贏得比賽的冠軍。

- She felt so surprised that she shed happy tears.

  = So surprised she felt that she shed happy tears.

  （→補為分詞surprised，搭配副詞so）

  她驚喜地留下快樂的眼淚。

- Such is Edward's eloquence that the many voters support his proposals.

  （→補語為Edward's eloquence，搭配形容詞such）

  愛德華口才很好，所以選民支持他的提案。

- Such a patient nurse was she that she was chosen as the role model for medical practitioners.

（→補語為a good girl，搭配形容詞such）

她是如此有耐心的護士，以至於被選為醫護人員的模範。

Test 快來即時測驗自己的學習成果吧！

( ) 1. _____ that she would definitely achieve her goal.
(A) Such is her determination　(B) Such determined girl
(C) She is such determined girl　(D) So determined she

( ) 2. Mandy was _____ that she wouldn't buy a lunch box for her younger brother.
(A) such stingy　　　　　(B) so stingy
(C) such stingy girl　　　(D) so much stingy

( ) 3. Helen takes up _____ she has to stay up to finish it.
(A) such work　　　　　(B) such task
(C) such a great number　(D) so much work

( ) 4. _____ that he decided to give up.
(A) So frustrated he felt　(B) Such frustration
(C) So frustrated he is　　(D) So much frustration

( ) 5. _____ the germs could all be killed.
(A) Such the temperature　(B) So high temperature
(C) Such high temperature　(D) The temperature was so high

解答：(A) (B) (D) (A) (B)

Part 9 | 表讓步的倒裝句型

1. 表示「縱然、即使」的句型，由although/though等放句首引導一般條件子句或由As放句中，以倒裝句的形式呈現。

2. 由as引導的倒裝句，句型為：

> adj. / 分詞/ 名詞+ as / though + S + V⋯
> = be + S + ever so + adj. ⋯

3. 口訣：**Although**放句首、**As**放句中、**N**之前無冠詞

- Although the soufflé is delicious, I could only have a bite of it.

   = Delicious as the soufflé is, I could only have a bite of it.

   = Be the soufflé so delicious, I could only have a bite if it.

   （→補語為adj. delicious）

   雖然這個舒芙蕾鬆餅很好吃，我也只能吃一小口。

- Even though she is a lazy girl, she is willing to complete the complex task.

   = Lazy girl as she is, she is willing to complete the complex task.

   （→補語為N a lazy girl，倒裝時需把冠詞a去掉）

   雖然她是個懶惰的女孩子，她還是願意完成這個複雜的任務。

- Though we are optimistic about the outcome, we have to be cautious in the process.

   = Optimistic as we are about the outcome, we have to be cautious in the process.

   （→補語為adj. optimistic）

   我們對結果雖然樂觀，但是對過程還是要很小心。

( ) 1. _____, she stayed up to finish the report.

(A) Although being tired

(B) Tired as she was

(C) Be so tired

(D) As tired as she

( ) 2. _____, he was fooled by the con artist.

(A) Though smart the professor was

(B) Smart though the professor

(C) As smart as the professor

(D) Be the profession so smart

( ) 3. _____, he couldn't get admitted to his ideal colleague.

(A) As hard-working as he was

(B) Hard-working as he was

(C) Be he so hard-working

(D) Though working hard

( ) 4. _____, the fisherman still went fishing.

(A) As harsh as the condition

(B) Although the harsh condition

(C) Be the condition so harsh

(D) Since the condition was so harsh

( ) 5. _____, Jerry solved it within one minute.

(A) Difficult question as it was

(B) As difficult a question as it was

(C) So difficult a question as it was

(D) Though difficult a question it was

解答：(B) (D) (B) (C) (A)

因主詞太長，而將主詞補語放句首而倒裝的句型。句型變化如下：

S＋beV＋SC (adj./V-ing/V-p.p.)

→ SC (adj./V-ing/V-p.p.)＋beV＋S...

補語置首，後接be動詞，最後是主詞。

- Such strange phenomenon is rarely seen.

  = Rarely seen is such strange phenomenon.

  這樣的怪現象很少看到。

- Those who are generous are admired.

  = Admired are those who are generous.

  慷慨的人會受到景仰。

- The celebrity's reputation is related to what he does.

  = Related to the celebrity's reputation is what he does.

  名人的聲譽和他的作為有關。

- She wrote in a familiar style.

  = In a familiar style she wrote.

  她用親切的筆調寫作。

- Your recent work has been below standard.

  = Below standard has been your recent work.

  你最近的工作一直低於標準。

- This machine was invented by him.

  = Invented by him was the machine.

  這台機器是他發明的。

Test 快來即時測驗自己的學習成果吧！

( ) 1. _____ those who stick to their goals.
    (A) Appreciated is   (B) Admired are
    (C) Suffering is   (D) To be respected

( ) 2._____ is nowhere else to be found.
    (A) Such bargain good
    (B) So a good bargain
    (C) Such a good bargain
    (D) So good bargain

( ) 3. _____ are those who volunteered to help others.
    (A) To bless   (B) Blessed   (C) So bless   (D) Such luck

( ) 4. _____ is the wild hawk.
    (A) Hardly find   (B) Rarely seen   (C) Seldom meet   (D) Often watch

( ) 5. _____ is the pop star's poster.
    (A) Commonly seen   (B) Widely spreading
    (C) Broadly print   (D) Generally heard

解答：(A) (D) (B) (B) (A)

Note

Part 11 方位副詞的倒裝句型

1. 將地方副詞（片語）置句首，是加強語氣的用法，目的在強調句子中的地方副詞（片語），其後之句子須將主詞和動詞的位置互換，不須用助動詞來形成倒裝句（亦即非問句式倒裝）。

2. 常用的地方副詞除了there、here 外，還有表示地方的介副詞，如：in、out、up down、off、way 等，以及表示位置的副詞片語，如：near my house、on the tree、in the church等。

- An old tree stood at the peak of the mountain.

  = At the peak of the mountain stood an old tree.
  山巔上矗立著一棵老樹。

- A concrete electric pole stood next to the building.

  = Next to the building stood a concrete electric pole.
  建築物旁邊立著一根電線桿。

- When she opened the door, out flew a sparrow.
  當她把門打開的時候，一隻麻雀飛了出來。

注意要點

在此句型中，若主詞為代名詞，則地方副詞（片語）之後不需倒裝。

Come on! There you go again.	拜託，你又來了。
Here you are.	給你。
Here we are.	我們到了。
There she goes.	她走了。
There goes the bell.	鈴響了。

有時也會將句子中的時間副詞移置句首，時間副詞之後亦須將主詞和動詞的位置互換，不需用助動詞來形成倒裝句。

- **Then comes the bear market.**
  然後股票市場下跌了。

- **After the storm comes a calm.**
  否極泰來。

Test 快來即時測驗自己的學習成果吧！

( ) 1. _____ a herd of sheep.

    (A) Down the hill came   (B) Came down the hill

    (C) Down the hill is   (D) Down the hill comes

( ) 2. _____ an old tree.

    (A) Stand near the house   (B) Beside the house stand

    (C) Stood behind the house   (D) Next to the house stands

( ) 3. When he came to the door, _____.

    (A) out a thief rush   (B) rushed out a thief

    (C) rushed a thief out   (D) out rushed a thief

( ) 4. _____ the oil price went. It became cheaper.

    (A) Up   (B) Down   (C) Forward   (D) Backward

( ) 5. _____ a church.

    (A) On the top of the hill is

    (B) Right next to the temple

    (C) Beside the office building can see

    (D) Next to the store can you find

解答：(A) (B) (D) (D) (A)

217

Part 12 假設語氣的倒裝句型

1. 假設語氣的倒裝常出現在文學作品中，因為順序有變，又省略掉關鍵字**if**，所以閱讀時需要仔細判讀。

2. 句型變化如下：

If + S + were …	Were + S
If + S + V…	Do / Does / Did + S + VR
If + S + V…	助V + S + VR

- If I were the prime minister, I could put more emphasis on social welfare.

  = Were I the prime minister, I would put more emphasis on the social welfare.

  如果我是首相，我就會更加重視社會福利。

- If he had got better prepared, he wouldn't have made a blunder.

  = Had he got better prepared, he wouldn't have made a blunder.

  如果他準備的好一點，他就不會犯這個錯誤。

- If she should change her mind, we will have to reschedule the meeting.

  = Should she change her mind, we will have to reschedule the meeting.

  如果她改變心意，我們就必須要重新安排會議時間。

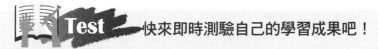

(　) 1. _____, we will cancel the flight.

(A) Should the weather get worse

(B) Worse as the weather condition become

(C) If the weather had become worse

(D) Should the weather have gotten worse

(　) 2. _____, he could offer us some useful advice.

(A) Were he an expert

(B) It he had been an expert

(C) Should he be an expert

(D) Had he been an expert

(　) 3. _____, she wouldn't have been late for work.

(A) Should she catch the bus

(B) Had she caught the bus

(C) If she catches

(D) If she had caught

(　) 4. _____, her mother would not be so angry.

(A) Should she tell the truth

(B) Should she tell the truth

(C) Has she told the truth

(D) If she told the truth

(　) 5. _____, he should go to see a doctor as soon as possible.

(A) If he shows signs of flu

(B) If he had flu symptoms

(C) Had he showed signs of flu

(D) Has he showed signs of flu

解答：(A) (D) (B) (A) (A)

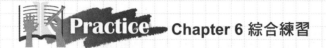

( ) 1. _____ that the questions in the jeopardy game were so difficult.

(A) Never had we heard   (B) We never know

(C) We never hear   (D) We will never know

( ) 2. By no means _____ the company's rules.

(A) we should violate   (B) violate we should

(C) should we violate   (D) we violate

( ) 3. _____ should you play such a dangerous trick on your friend.

(A) Scarcely   (B) Under no circumstance

(C) By all means   (D) In every aspect

( ) 4. Only when the passenger feels safe _____.

(A) can he fall asleep   (B) should they get onboard

(C) was he satisfied   (D) will they feel calm

( ) 5. Only by folding the paper _____ my pocket.

(A) can I fit it   (B) can it be fit into

(C) can I make it fit into   (D) can it fit into

( ) 6. No sooner had he seen the police officer _____.

(A) before running away   (B) when he runs away

(C) than he ran away   (D) did he run

( ) 7. _____ the model of dinosaur, the kid yelled with excitement.

(A) Upon seeing   (B) No sooner had he seen

(C) The moment he sees   (D) Hardly had he seen

( ) 8. _____ that they arrived at their destination.

(A) No sooner than midnight   (B) It was not until midnight

(C) Not until it was midnight   (D) It is until midnight

( ) 9. _____ did he have the right to vote.

(A) Not until he was 18   (B) It was not until last year

(C) Not until 18 years old   (D) It was until last year

( ) 10. _____, the water is to the fish.

(A) As to me art is   (B) Art is to me

(C) What art is to me   (D) As art is to me

( ) 11. _____ clean the house, but she also cooked dinner for us.

(A) However does Rose   (B) Not only did Rose

(C) Although Rose does   (D) Though she

( ) 12. _____, the workers will complete the construction work.

(A) Were it so difficult

(B) Difficult though the situation

(C) Be it so difficult

(D) Despite of the difficult situation

( ) 13. _____, nor would he offer suggestions.

(A) Neither did he share the burden

(B) He would either take responsibility

(C) Neither he took responsibility

(D) Either would he share the burden

( ) 14. _____ that all children in the orphanage got a Christmas gift from him.

(A) So generous is she   (B) Such generosity he has

(C) She is so generous   (D) Such a generous person

( ) 15. _____ the visiting professor on campus, we should show courtesy to her.

(A) If we will see   (B) Had we seen

(C) If we had seen   (D) Should we see

Chapter 7
It的相關句型

Part 1 | it 作虛主詞與補語

1. It is＋adj.＋(for sb.)＋to V

1. 當虛主詞 **it** 代替真主詞不定詞片語、不定詞片語作主詞用時，須搭配單數動詞。句型為**It is＋adj.＋(for sb.)＋to V**，表示「對某人而言，做某件事情是……的。」

2. 此句型中的形容詞，是所謂的「非人形容詞」，用來修飾後面的不定詞，而不是修飾人，所以不可以改成用人做主詞。

3. 這類形容詞有：

　　(1)（重要的）important/crucial/significant
　　(2)（必要的）necessary/imperative/essential
　　(3)（不必要的）unnecessary
　　(4)（困難的）hard/difficult
　　(5)（容易的）easy
　　(6)（方便的）convenient
　　(7)（不方便的）inconvenient
　　(8)（緊急的）urgent/emergent

- It is necessary for people who are allergic to seafood to watch their diet.
  對海鮮過敏的人注意飲食是必要的。

- It is inconvenient for me to commute from the suburb to the downtown.
  從郊區通勤到市中心對我來說很不方便。

- It is crucial for passengers to fill out the declaration form.
  旅客填寫申報單是必要的。

- It is urgent for us to get rid of the glitches in the production line.
  處理好產線上面的故障是很緊急的。

    本句型也可以與It is important/necessary…＋that＋S＋(should)＋V 的句型互換。

- It is essential for each of us to monitor our own mental health condition.

  = It is essential that we watch our own mental health condition.
  我們每個人都必須監測自己的心理健康狀態，這是基本而必要的。

- It is urgent that we (should) make the unleashed dog calm down.
  我們應該馬上讓拖離牽繩的狗冷靜下來。

Test 快來即時測驗自己的學習成果吧！

( ) 1. It is unnecessary _____ you to worry about that stranger.
    (A) for   (B) that   (C) with   (D) from

( ) 2. It is imperative _____ we change our schedule because of the natural disaster.
    (A) with   (B) to   (C) for   (D) that

( ) 3. It was necessary for us _____ our report before handing it out.
    (A) proofreads   (B) proofreading   (C) to proofread   (D) proofread

( ) 4. It is imperative that passengers _____ their packages checked.
    (A) to have   (B) should have   (C) for having   (D) will have

( ) 5. It is emergent _____ us to call an ambulance.
    (A) for   (B) that   (C) to   (D) with

解答：(A) (D) (C) (B) (A)

2. It is ＋ adj. ＋ of sb. ＋ to V

1. 此類的形容詞是用來修飾人的，而不是修飾事物，所以可以把整句改成人作主詞。

2. 這類形容詞有：凡是可以修飾人的形容詞，都可以如此使用。

    (1)（好心的）good/kind/kind-hearted、

       （有同情心的）sympathetic

    (2)（殘忍的）cruel

    (3)（有禮貌的）polite/well-mannered、（無禮的）impolite/rude

- It is kind of her to take care of the homeless dogs.
  = She is kind to take care of the homeless dogs.
  她照顧無家可歸的狗，真是好心。

- It is unkind of him to gossip about his colleagues.
  = He is unkind to gossip about his colleagues.
  他這樣說同事的八卦，真是很壞心。

- It is cruel of that man to abuse his pet dog.
  他虐待寵物狗，真是殘忍。

注意要點

注意下面兩句中，因不同的介系詞而讓good有不同含意。

- It is good for you to read more finance books.
  （→good修飾事物）
  閱讀財金書籍對你是很好的。

- It is good of you to offer advice for me.
  （→good修飾人）
  你真是心地善良，會提供我建議。

3. It is＋a/the/one's＋N＋that...

1. 本章到此為止的句型中，**it**都做虛主詞，有時是指後面的不定詞片語，有時是指**that**子句。在本句型中，**that**後面所加上的子句，其實就是用來說明前面名詞的補語，因此，**that**後面是一個完整的子句。

2. 在這個句型中，**that**是用來引導後面補充說明**that**之前的名詞子句，所以不能用其他關係代名詞替代。

- It was a surprise that my friend sent me a flower bouquet on my birthday. （→這裡的**that**之後，是一個完整子句。用來補充說明前面的驚喜。）
  我朋友在我生日時我一束花，真是驚喜。

3. 另外，常混淆的是分裂強調句，請看以下句子：

- It was a flower bouquet that my friend sent me on my birthday.
  （→這裡的**that**是代替前面的**a flower bouquet**。**that**之後的句子應該是**my friend sent me on my birthday** ，於是可以知道是分裂強調句的寫法，這裡的**that**之後的子句是形容詞子句。）
  我朋友在生日時送我的是一束花。

- It was his ideal that his students can become self-independent.
  他的理想是他的學生可以自我獨立。（→名詞子句）

- It is established that those with self-discipline are more likely to succeed.
  有自律的人比較可能成功，這是個既定的事實。（→名詞子句）

- It was a heart-warming story that he told on the program.
  = It was a heart-warming story which he told on the program.
  當時他在節目上說的是個溫馨的故事。（→強調句型）

- It was a terrible trick that he played on his classmate.
  他對同學做的是個很糟糕的惡作劇。（→強調句型）

若是為that引導補語的句型，可與下列句型互相替換。

- It is our belief that she is great assistant for the manager.
  = We believe that she is a great assistant for the manager.
  = It is believed that she is a great assistant for the manager.
  = She is believed to be a great assistant for the manager.
  我們相信她會是經理很好的助手。

Test 快來即時測驗自己的學習成果吧！

( ) 1. It is generous _____ you to share your experience with me.

    (A) for   (B) to   (C) of   (D) with

( ) 2. It is impolite _____ him to use foul language on the meeting.

    (A) with   (B) to   (C) for   (D) of

( ) 3. It is cruel of her _____ speak ill of her little sister.

    (A) to   (B) that   (C) for   (D) with

( ) 4. It is necessary _____ him to get rid of his bad habit.

    (A) to   (B) for   (C) of   (D) with

( ) 5. It is sympathetic of her _____ help that old lady carry the heavy baggage.

    (A) by   (B) to   (C) for   (D) with

解答：(C) (D) (A) (B) (B)

Part 2 | 分裂強調句型

1. 句型要點：為加強句中某部份語氣而使用之結構

It is / was + 被強調的結構 + that 子句

sth.　　　　that / which
地方副詞.　　where
時間副詞　　when

It is/was...that...屬於分裂句，可以強調主詞、受詞、時間副詞、地方副詞等。另外，除了用that之外，也可以依據前面強調的語詞，使用適當的關係代名詞(who/whom/whose/which)，或關係副詞(when/where)等。

2. It is a＋N that...這種句型，後面的句子為完整的子句，用來作為前面名詞的補語，相當於名詞的同位語。

- It was Laurie that spread the rumor in the department last month.
  上個月是蘿莉在部門裡傳播謠言的。

- It was a rumor that Laurie spread in the department last month.
  上個月蘿莉在部門裡散佈的是個謠言。

- It was in the department that Laurie spread a rumor.
  上個月蘿莉是在部門裡散布謠言的。

- It was last month that Laurie spread the rumor in the department.
  蘿莉是上個月在部門裡散布謠言的。

- It was in mid-autumn afternoon when/that we first visited the campus of my ideal college.
  在一個秋天的下午，我們第一次造訪了我理想大學的校園。

- It was my cousin who/that offered financial support when I was in trouble.
  當我陷入麻煩時，是我的堂哥給我經濟的援助。

• It was not until two months later that we completed that survey.
直到兩個月之後，我們才完成這個調查。

注意要點

　　動詞不可以用分裂句強調，而是要用助動詞＋原形動詞來強調。

• The client's lukewarm attitude did discouraged me at that moment.
顧客不冷不熱的態度，當時的確讓我覺得失望。

• The outcome of the research did astonished the scientists.
研究的結果的確讓科學家震驚。

Test ——快來即時測驗自己的學習成果吧！

( ) 1. It was my coworker _____ told me the change in the office etiquette.
(A) that　　(B) when　　(C) which　　(D) what

( ) 2. It was in the hospital _____ my mother was cured last year.
(A) when　　(B) who　　(C) where　　D) how

( ) 3. Jenny _____ when she forgot her supervisor's name.
(A) did feel embarrassed　　(B) was embarrassing
(C) did embarrass　　(D) were embarrassed

( ) 4. It was my uncle _____ reminded me to be more cautious about making investment.
(A) then　　(B) which　　(C) who　　(D) how

( ) 5. It was in 1999 _____ Kevin produced in his first movie.
(A) how　　(B) when　　(C) who　　(D) where

解答：(A) (C) (A) (C) (B)

Part 3 | 以it為虛主詞，that子句為真主詞的句型

 1. that 子句為真主詞的基本概念

1. 在這個句型裡，**it**為虛主詞，真正的主詞為**that**引導的名詞子句。主詞為名詞子句時常以虛主詞 **it**代替，把名詞子句置於形容詞後面以避免頭重腳輕。**that**不可省略。

2. that子句中的主詞可移到句首，之後接不定詞來描述現況或事實。若**that**子句的時間早於主要子句表示事情已發生，則要用不定詞完成式。

3. 除了不定詞和不定詞完成式，表示動作正在進行要用 **to＋be＋V-ing**，表被動語態時則用 **to＋be＋V-p.p.** 或 **to＋have＋been＋V-p.p.**。

- That a burglar broke into the house was obvious, because all things were in a mess. （→無虛主詞it情況）

  = It was obvious that a burglar broke into the house because all things were in a mess. （→有虛主詞it情況）

  顯然有小偷闖進房子裡，因為東西都亂七八糟的。

- That the figure skater would get the highest score is predictable. （→無虛主詞it情況）

  = It is predictable that the figure skater would get the highest score. （→有虛主詞it情況）

  可以預測到這位花式溜冰選手會得到最高分。

- It turned out that Ed was the supporter of the charity foundation. （→有虛主詞it情況）

  = Ed turned out to be the supporter of the charity foundation. （→無虛主詞it情況）

  原來艾德就是慈善機機會的贊助者。

- It seems that Mia could not follow the lecturer on the seminar.

  = Mia seems to have difficulty following the lecturer on the seminar.

  米亞似乎跟不上研討會上的講師。

- It seems that Sean is negotiating with the customer.

  = Sean seems to be negotiating with the customer.

  尚恩似乎在和顧客協商。

- It seemed that the meeting minutes was completed by James alone.

  = The meeting minutes seemed to have been completed by James alone.

  似乎會議記錄已經由詹姆士一個人完成了。

　　此句型的主詞除了名詞外，也可用 it 來代替名詞子句（that子句、wh-子句、whether/if子句）。也可用 a big、a great、a little、little、some 等取代 no，表示影響的程度。

- Whether the concert will be postponed has a lot to do with the weather.

  = It has a lot to do with the weather whether the concert will be postponed.

  演唱會是否延期視天氣而定。

- It made some difference that the he tried to compensate to loss.

  他試圖彌補損失，多少有些幫助。

❶ 在此句型裡，除了 be 動詞、become 外，也可用 seem、appear（似乎）等動詞，表示語氣不是十分肯定。

- It appears that the refugee will get humanitarian aid.

  難民似乎會獲得人道救援。

- It seems that the contract terms are acceptable for the client.

  合約條文對客戶來說似乎是可以接受的。

- With the analysis of the soil sample, it appeared that the land is contaminated with chemicals.

  根據對土壤樣本的分析，土地似乎受到化學物質污染了。

❷ It matters/doesn't matter (to sb.) that/whether/if＋子句（有關係／沒關係）與此句型有類似的意思。

- **It matters whether everyone will attend the meeting because the manager will make a significant accouchement.**
  是否每個人都參與這次會議很重要，因為經理會做出重大的宣布。

- **Does it matter that she didn't show her personal preference?**
  她沒有表示個人喜好有關係嗎？

- **It matters to me whether my sister could attend my wedding banquet.**
  我妹妹能否出席我的婚宴對我很重要。

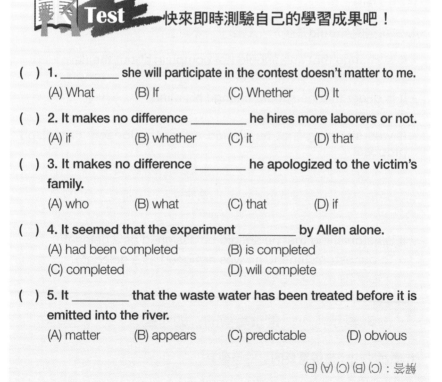

Test ──快來即時測驗自己的學習成果吧！

( ) 1. _____ she will participate in the contest doesn't matter to me.

    (A) What   (B) If   (C) Whether   (D) It

( ) 2. It makes no difference _____ he hires more laborers or not.

    (A) if   (B) whether   (C) it   (D) that

( ) 3. It makes no difference _____ he apologized to the victim's family.

    (A) who   (B) what   (C) that   (D) if

( ) 4. It seemed that the experiment _____ by Allen alone.

    (A) had been completed   (B) is completed
    (C) completed   (D) will complete

( ) 5. It _____ that the waste water has been treated before it is emitted into the river.

    (A) matter   (B) appears   (C) predictable   (D) obvious

解答：(C) (B) (C) (A) (B)

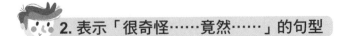 **2. 表示「很奇怪……竟然……」的句型**

1. 一個句子的主詞若過長時，可用虛主詞it代替，並以that子句為真正的主詞。**that**子句中的主詞可移到句首，之後接不定詞來描述現況或事實。若 that 子句的時間早於主要子句表示事情已發生，則要用不定詞完成式。

2. 本句型要以形容詞表示「令人驚訝的、怪異的、奇異的」。句型為：

　　It is surprising/strange/unbelievable＋that＋S＋should＋VR

3. 適用於這種句型的相關形容詞：**queer**（奇怪的）、**astonishing**（令人驚訝的）、**incredible**（令人難以置信的）、**stunning**（令人目瞪口呆的）等。

4. 本句型的**should**是表示「竟然」，不可省略。

- It is strange that she should not complain about the flaw.
  她竟然沒有抱怨這個瑕疵，真是奇怪。

- It is queer that he should change his mind.
  他竟然會改變心意，也太奇怪了。

- It was stunning that he should adopt the loosely-organized proposal.
  令人目瞪口呆的是，他竟然會接受這麼結構鬆散的提案。

　　這個句型可以替換成to one's ＋ 情緒性名詞，意為「令（人）……的」。

- It is astonishing that he should be assigned as a delegate.
  = To our astonishment, he was assigned as a delegate.
  令人驚訝地，他竟然被指定為代表。

 3. 表示「……是很重要的」的句型

1. 表示「……是很重要的」的句型為：

　　It is important/essential/crucial＋that＋S＋(should)＋VR。

本句型是由It is＋adj.＋for＋sb.＋to＋V演變而來的。
也可以代換成：It is important for＋sb.＋to＋V

2. 適用於這種句型的相關形容詞常表「重要的、急迫的、必須的、義務的」等意思，如：crucial、essential、imperative、important、necessary、obligatory、urgent、vital 等。

- It is important that he should plan his itinerary in advance.
  = It is important for him to plan his itinerary in advance.
  他必須要事先規劃行程，這是很重要的。

- It is vital that an English learner has lots of input of the language.
  英語學習者要大量接觸這種語言，這是很重要的。

- It is important that everyone follow the etiquette on the award ceremony.
  在頒獎典禮上，每個人都要遵守禮節，這是很重要的。

  It is＋adj.＋of＋sb.＋to＋V的句型則不可以改成It is adj.＋that＋S (should)＋V的句型。

- It is kind of you to volunteer to clean the beach.
  = You are kind to volunteer to clean the beach.
  你自願去清理海灘真是好。

延伸學習

在現代英文中，that 子句也常用直述句來表示。

- It is imperative that all team members work together to achieve the goal.
  所有的團隊成員需要合作達成目標。

- It is obligatory that a report is handed in to the HR director when an employee is taking a long leave.
  員工要請長假的時候，需要繳交報告給人事主任。

( ) 1. It is stunning that the police officer _____ the pickpocket without even questioning him.

(A) will release　(B) releasing　(C) should release　(D) releases

( ) 2. It was incredible that Caldarella's foot _____ in the glass stiletto.

(A) fitting　(B) fitted　(C) fit　(D) should fit

( ) 3. It is necessary that passengers _____ the card when entering the station.

(A) swipe　(B) swipes　(C) swiped　(D) will swipe

( ) 4. It is urgent that you _____ the habit of procrastinating.

(A) will quit　(B) to be quit　(C) quitted　(D) should quit

( ) 5. It was unbelievable that the little boy _____ the broccoli in the launch box.

(A) should eat up　(B) eat up　(C) eater up　(D) will eat up

解答：(C) (D) (A) (D) (A)

4. 表達「據說」的句型

1. 表示「據說……」的句型為：

It is said/believed/reported/rumored...that＋S＋V
據說／一般相信／據報導／諸傳……等

2. 此句型用來表達客觀的立場，代替其後之名詞子句，**that**不可省略。

3. 其他可用的動詞包括：**said**、**believed**、**thought**、**reported**、**expected**、**rumored** 等，須注意文意差異。

4. 這個句型有幾種變化，要特別注意。

❶ 如果用it做虛主詞時，要用被動，表示後面那件事是被說／被報導／被謠傳等。

❷ 如果用人如：people或they作主詞需用主動。

❸ 若後子句中主詞做真主詞時，則其後要使用不定詞，不可加 that子句。

5. 上述的句型變化，轉換時要注意前後子句的時態是否一致。如果後面的事實時代比較早，則變成不定詞時，需使用**to have＋V-p.p.**的型態。

6. 除了用虛主詞**It**代替**that** 子句外，也可將子句中的主詞移到句首接不定詞，即：**S＋be reported/said＋to＋V**。

• People say that he is brave.

= It is said that he is brave.

= He is said to be brave.

聽說他很勇敢。

• People say that he was brave.

= It is said that he was brave.

= He is said to have been brave.

聽說他曾經很勇敢。

• It is reported that Greenland's ice sheet is melting because of global warming.

= Greenland's ice sheet is said to be melting because of global warming.

據報導格陵蘭島的冰層因為全球暖化正在融化。

• It is said that he rescued a lot of wild animals when he was young.

= He is said to have rescued a lot of wild animals when he was young.

據說他年輕時拯救過很多野生動物。

• It is said that it took James nearly two weeks to assemble the model yacht.

據說詹姆士花了將近兩個星期組裝這個遊艇模型。

• It was expected that the flight would be canceled because of the severe weather.

班機預期會被取消，因為天氣狀況太差了。

1. that 子句為 it 的同位語，word、rumor、legend、tradition要用單數，且不加冠詞。

- **It is rumored that the superstar was lip-syncing on her live concert.** 據説這位巨星在她的現場演唱會上對嘴。

- **Legend has it that pointing at the moon with you index finger will bring bad luck.**
  據説用食指指月亮會帶來壞運。

2. It is rumored that...也可代換為Rumor has it that...，表示「據説；傳聞」。

- **Rumor has it that the board had prearranged his promotion.** 據説董事會已經預先安排了他的升遷。

- **It is rumored that the politician is having an affair with his secretary.**
  謠傳那個政治人物和他的秘書外遇。

3. it 為虛主詞代替 that 子句，可改成 S＋be well-known＋for sth. 的形式。

  It is a well-known＋N＋that＋S＋V 亦是常見的句型。

- **It is well-known that a nanny should have some nursing knowledge.**
  = A nanny is well-known to have some nursing knowledge.
  大家都知道保姆會有一些護理的知識。

- **It's a well-known fact that solar power can generate electricity.**
  太陽能可以用來發電是大家都知道的。

4. 類似的句型 It is universally/widely/generally acknowledged 表「普世公認的」。

- **It is universally acknowledged that the Earth's petroleum reserves would become fully exhausted someday.**
  地球的石油存量有一天會耗盡是大家都知道的。

( ) 1. It is _____ that sea turtles are endangered because their habitat is being damaged.

(A) rumor　　(B) said　　　　(C) well-known　(D) to report

( ) 2. It is _____ that a typhoon might hit the island next month.

(A) said　　　(B) expect　　　　(C) prediction　(D) famous

( ) 3. He is said _____ stingy when he was young.

(A) that he was　(B) to have been　(C) to be　　(D) used to be

( ) 4. Rumor has it that the chief judge _____ a certain player in the contest.

(A) favor　(B) would have favored　(C) to favor　(D) favors

( ) 5. It is said that he _____ a mansion in the suburbs, and he keeps eleven golden retrievers there.

(A) had had　(B) has　　(C) having　　(D) should have

解答：(C) (A) (B) (D) (B)

5. 表達「的確……但……」的句型

1. **It is true that..., but** 用來前後語意相反的句子，可用 **yet** 代替，表示「的確……但……」，此句型較常用於口語中。

2. **It is true that** 亦可用肯定副詞如 **surely**、**certainly**、**indeed** 代替。

3. 此句型可改成 **the truth is that..., but...**，**but** 前會用逗號與前面句子隔開。

● Certainly I'd like to help you, but I have to revise my proposal first.
  = Indeed, I'd like to help you, but I have to revise my proposal first.
  = It is true that I'd like to help you, but I have to revise my proposal first.
  = The truth is that I'd like to help you, but I have to revise my proposal first. 我真的想幫忙你，但是我必須先修改我的提案。

● It is true that he's an eloquent speaker, but he's not dedicated to lecturing. 他是個口才很好的演說者，不過他不熱愛演說。

Part 4 | 其他it 為虛主詞的句型

 1. 表達「……是值得的」句型

1. 要表達「……是值得的」有主要下列句型

❶ It pays to VR...

在此句型中，it為虛主詞，且是固定的用法，不能將to＋VR挪前成為主詞。

- **It pays to studying and doing part-time jobs at the same time.**
  半工半讀是值得的。

❷ worth＋N/V-ing

worth之後接名詞或V-ing，接名詞表示「值多少金錢或所花的代價（時間或努力）是值得的」，而 V-ing 的用法，不分主被動，都直接加V-ing。

- **If you get the chance, the Times Square in New York is worth visiting.**
  = If you get the chance, the Times Square in New York is worth a visit.
  如果你有機會，紐約的時報廣場值得去看看。

- **It is absolutely worth your time to hang out with a talented writer.**
  花時間和一位有才華的作家相處是絕對值得的事情。

❸ worthy＋of N/to V

worthy之後可接 of＋N 或 to V，表示「值得……的；配得上」的意思。worthy 之後表主動用 of＋V-ing 或 to＋V，表被動用 of＋being＋V-p.p.或 to be＋V-p.p.，不過這種用法複雜且少見，不建議使用。

- He has no experience. He isn't worthy of being given the job.

  = He has no experience. He isn't worthy to be given the job.

  他沒有經驗，他配不上接受這份工作。

- The town is worthy of note because a famous author was born here.

  這個城鎮值得注意，因為曾有一名著名的作家出生在這裡。

❹ It is worthwhile＋to V/V-ing

　　本句型還可以It is worthwhile＋to V表示。worthwhile 之後可接 to＋V或V-ing，It 用來代替真正的主詞 to＋V 或 V-ing。

- It is worthwhile to follow the docent at the museum, for he would give a thorough illustration of the exhibits.

  = It is worthwhile following the docent at the museum, for he would give a thorough illustration of the exhibits.

  在博物館跟著一位導覽員走很值得，因為他會詳細解說陳列品。

- It is worthwhile for young people like you to pay a visit to the world heritage sites.

  = It is worthwhile for young people like you paying a visit to the world heritage sites.

  = Paying a visit to the world heritage sites is worthwhile for young people like you.

  像你們這樣的年輕人，去參觀世界遺產是很值得的。

延伸學習

1. pay除了用於上面的句型以外，也常用來指「付錢」。注意下面的分別：

　　❶ pay＋sb.　　　付錢給……

　　❷ pay for＋sth.　　付錢買（某物）

　　❸ pay the bill/tuition/rent　　付帳／學費／租金

　　❹ pay one's way through college　　半工半讀唸完大學

- **To my embarrassment, I forgot to pay the monthly utility bill.** 令我很尷尬的是，我忘了繳月電費。
- **How much did you pay for the switch ring fit?** 你花了多少錢買那個健身環？

2. worthwhile 值得的 worth one's while 來強調「值得某人……」，one's 可省略。

- **It is worth your while to consult the mentor about your career choice.** 向你的導師諮詢職涯選擇是值得的。

3. 本句型也可以替換成：It is rewarding＋to V。

- **It is rewarding to have the trial-and-error experience.** 有這個嘗試錯誤的經驗是值得的。

4.「值……時間、金錢」也可用「數量所有格＋worth of sth.」來表示。

- **The burglar stole away ten thousand dollars' worth of gold.** 小偷偷走了價值一萬元的黃金。

Test ——快來即時測驗自己的學習成果吧！

( ) 1. To me, it is worthwhile _____ my time in experiments, for experience is the best teacher.

(A) devoting　(B) for devoting　(C) devote　(D) devotion

( ) 2. Seeing the action movie in a theater is _____ for a fan of Kong Fu movies.

(A) worthy　(B) reward　(C) worthwhile　(D) worth

( ) 3. It is rewarding _____ with a veteran worker like Jack.

(A) taking　(B) talked　(C) to talk　(D) talks

( ) 4. It's _____ standing in line for three hours to purchase this limited-edition figurine.

(A) worthwhile (B) worthy   (C) worth   (D) worthy

( ) 5. The inspiring short talk is _____ of forwarding to your friend.

(A) worthwhile (B) worthy   (C) worth   (D) worths

解答：(A) (C) (C) (C) (B)

2. 表達「突然想到……」的句型

1. 要表達「突然想到……」，有下列句型：

It strikes / occurs to + sb. + to V / that 子句
= sb. hit on the idea that＋子句

2. 此句型中的it是虛主詞，後接現在式或過去式動詞，但以過去式較為常見。

3. 動詞前面可加上副詞 **never** 或 **suddenly** 來修飾或加強語氣。

4. 寫作時需注意其動詞之三態變化：

❶ hit/hit/hit

❷ strike/struck/struck (stricken)

❸ occur/occurred/occurred

• When I was watching the television sitcom, it occurred to me that I had not finished reviewing the lessons.
當我看電視影集的時候，忽然想到我還沒複習完功課。

• He hit on the idea that he should show more respect to the aboriginal culture.
他突然想到他應該對原住民文化表現出更多的尊敬之意。

• How did it occur to you that a hidden trap could be installed in the yard?
你是怎麼想到院子裡可能有裝設隱形的陷阱？

- **It never occurred to me that the new corona virus could cause public anxiety.**
  我從沒想到這個新型冠狀病毒會引起大眾焦慮。

＊that 子句的主詞可移到句首，之後接不定詞。

- **It happened that I saw a broadcast journalist at the local supermarket.**
  = **I happened to see a broadcast journalist at the local supermarket.**
  我在本地超市的時候看到一位廣播記者。

延伸學習

1. 下列句型亦可表「突然想到……」

(1) It crosses sb's mind that...
(2) It comes across sb's mind that...
(3) It pops into sb's mind that...
(4) It dawns on＋sb. that... 某人突然頓悟到……
(5) N＋flash into one's mind that... 某人突然想到……

- **It dawned on me that many successful people have a motto or principles to follow.**
  我突然頓悟到，許多成功的人都有座右銘或者要尊崇的原則。

- **An idea for the new novel flashed into his mind.**
  一個新小說的想法閃進他的腦海。

2. 上面的句型，也可以替換成：

sb.＋hit/strike upon the idea＋that＋子句＋of＋V-ing

- **Georgina hit on the idea that she could open a pet hotel.**
  = **It occurred to Georgina that she could open a pet hotel.**
  喬吉娜忽然想到她可以開一間寵物旅館。

3. 句型中的**happen to V** 的主詞為人時，表示「碰巧」。句型中的**happen to V** 的主詞為事物時，**sth. happens to sb./sth.** 表示「某人發生某事」或「某事發生什麼狀況」，表示「發生」。

- **If you happen to have a lawn mower, please lend it to me.**
  如果你正好有一台除草機，請把它借給我。
- **The boy is sitting on the stair weeping. I wonder what has happened to him.**
  小男孩坐在階梯上面哭泣，我納悶他發生什麼事了。

Test 快來即時測驗自己的學習成果吧！

( ) 1. It _____ that I could ask my cousin how to get rid of the glitches on my computer.
  (A) hit upon the idea   (B) occurred to me
  (C) came up with the idea (D) happened to

( ) 2. Jenny _____ that she could add coriander into the dough to make cookies.
  (A) happened to   (B) occurred to
  (C) hit upon the idea (D) struck the idea

( ) 3. It _____ that I forgot to return the electric cooker to my aunt.
  (A) was stricken   (B) occurred to me
  (C) happened   (D) hit on the idea

( ) 4. Johnson _____ that he could make a forehead thermometer by himself.
  (A) struck the idea (B) happened to
  (C) occurred   (D) hit on the idea

( ) 5. It never _____ that he would marry a woman who is 12 years older than him.
  (A) came across mind (B) occurred to him
  (C) happened to him   (D) hit on the idea

解答：(B) (C) (B) (D) (B)

3. 表達「……是無用的」句型

1. It is (of) no use＋V-ing.= It is useless＋to V. 表示「做某件事是無用的」，其中的**of**可省略。不論是**It is no use**或**It is of no use**，後面都可以加上動名詞或不定詞，兩者都正確。

2. 此句型還可代換為**There is no use＋(in)＋V-ing**，其中的 **in** 可省略。

- It is (of) no use forcing him to tell the secret.
  想強迫他說出秘密是沒有用的。

- It is no use crying over spilt milk.
  覆水難收。（後悔無用）

- There is no point/use in trying to meddle with his decision.
  = It is pointless/useless to try to meddle with his decision.
  試圖干涉他的決定是沒用的。

- There is no use in pouring water to a burning frying pot.
  用水去潑一個燒起來的鍋子是徒勞無功的。

- There/It is no use in thinking that you can always find someone to amend the mistake for you.
  認為你總是可以找到人來幫你彌補錯誤是沒有用的。

延伸學習

1. there is no＋V-ing 表示「……是不可能的；無法……」，與 it is impossible to＋V 意思相同。

- **There is no knowing whether he could make profit from his new business.**
  他是否能從新的生意當中獲利根本無從得知。

- **There is no denying that Helen makes the best risotto in town.**

  = It is impossible to deny that Helen makes the best risotto in town.
  不可否認，海倫做的燉飯是鎮上最好吃的。

2. 注意以下的區別：

❶ There is no use＋to V
　　= It is (of) no use＋V-ing/to V ……是沒有用的

❷ There is no need＋to V　　沒有必要去做……

❸ It is no wonder that...　　難怪……

❹ It goes without saying that...
　　=It is needless to say that... 不用說，……

❺ There is no doubt that...　　無疑地，……

❻ There is no point in＋V-ing　　　……是沒意義的

3. 禁止標語常用 no＋V-ing 或 no＋N 來表示，如：No Smoking、No Parking。

• **The sign says "No parking," so we'd better move our car to another place.**
這個標語上寫著「請勿停車」，所以我們最好把車移往他處。

4. 表達「花費了……」句型

1. 花費的對象，一個是錢，一個是時間，以下是相對應的句型：

❶ It takes (sb.) time＋to V　花時間／勞力等

❷ It costs (sb.) money＋to V　花錢

❸ sb. spend time/money on＋N/(in)＋V-ing

2. 以所花費的種類來區分時，cost只能用於「花費金錢」，spend都可用於「花費時間、金錢」，而take可用於非金錢可計價的花費。若以動詞的主詞來區分，cost跟take的主詞可以是人或事情，或用虛主詞it來代替，而spend 只能以人作為主詞。

3. spend 之後可接「**in＋動名詞**」或「**on＋名詞**」，介系詞 **in** 可以省略。

4. 注意動詞三態變化：

    ❶ take/took/taken

    ❷ cost/cost/cost

    ❸ spend/spent/spent

- **It will cost you about NT$10,000 to buy a Kindle electronic reader.**
  買台Kindle電子閱讀器大約要花台幣一萬元。

- **The sportscar cost him a fortune.**
  那輛跑車讓他花了一大筆錢。

- **It takes him about 40 minutes to commute to work every day.**
  = It takes about 40 minutes for him to commute to work every day.
  他每天花大約40分鐘通勤去工作。

- **He spent most of his savings on buying the house.**
  他把大部分的積蓄花在買房子上。

- **Some teenagers spend a lot of money on brand-name accessories.**
  有些青少年花很多錢在買名牌飾品上面。

- **Because of the poor Internet connection, it took James hours to upload the video clip to the cloud drive.**
  因為網路連線品質不好，詹姆士花了好幾個小時才將影片上傳到雲端空間。

延伸學習

    waste的用法和spend相同，意思是「浪費」。

- **You are not supposed to comment on his decision.**
  你不應該評論他的決定。

- **You are wasting your breath trying to convince her to leave her hot-tempered husband.**
  你想要勸她離開脾氣暴躁的丈夫，根本是白費力氣。

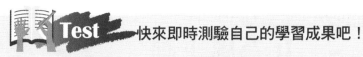

 Test 快來即時測驗自己的學習成果吧！

( ) 1. There is no use _____ to fix the severely damaged car.
(A) that trying (B) trying   (C) to try   (D) your try

( ) 2. It is not use _____ in advance for the boss is always changing his mind.
(A) for making plans   (B) we plan
(C) to make plans   (D) making plans

( ) 3. There is no point _____ direct mail ads for they are often ignored by shoppers.
(A) have sent (B) to send   (C) sending   (D) we send

( ) 4. It would cost him 80 thousand dollars _____ his office renovated.
(A) to have   (B) having   (C) that he had (D) for having

( ) 5. It took Gary three hours _____ with the client about the terms in the contract.
(A) for negotiating   (B) to negotiate
(C) negotiating   (D) that he negotiated

解答：(B) (D) (C) (A) (B)

ch 7 It 的相關句型

Note

Part **5** | It 為虛主詞的句型

1. 虛受詞的出現，常與S＋V＋O＋OC連用，其實與虛主詞有異曲同工之妙。當受詞太長，會使得受詞補語的位置拖到太後面而模糊焦點，所以用虛受詞的句型，以方便判讀受詞補語。

2. 以it為虛受詞的句型之一，用來表示「使人……覺得某事」的句型：

> S.（人）＋believe/consider/find/prove/think＋it＋adj.＋to＋V

3. 句型中的 it 為虛受詞，代替真正受詞的不定詞片語，這類動詞含有「認為」的意思，包括：**believe**、**consider**、**find**、**prove**、**think** 等。欲表明對象時，則在不定詞前加上 **for sb./sth.**。這個句型中的形容詞，就是前面所提到的「非人形容詞」，所以句中的it是代替後面不定詞的虛受詞。真正的受詞，是後面不定詞所說的事。

- Most people find it annoying to take the subway during the rush hour.
  多數人覺得在上下班尖峰時間搭乘地鐵是很煩人的。

- I think it rude for people to yawn when others are talking to you.
  我認為別人對你說話時打哈欠是很粗魯的。

4. 句型中的受詞補語可用名詞，不定詞也可改成 **that** 子句，**that** 可省略。

- Scientists have proven it unhealthy to consume too much sugar.
  = Scientists have proven (that) it is unhealthy to consume too much sugar.
  科學家證明吃太多糖是不健康的。

5. 此句型中的主詞不明確或不重要時，亦可改成被動語態。

- In India, it is considered inauspicious to eat beef.
  在印度，吃牛肉被認為是一種不祥的事。

延伸學習

1. 以 it 為虛受詞的句型之一，用來表示「注重……、養成……的習慣」的句型：

❶ S（人）＋make it a rule＋to V
= S（人）＋make a rule of＋V-ing

❷ S（人）＋make it a point＋to V
= S（人）＋make a point of＋V-ing

- I make it a habit to watch a piece of English news.
  = I make it a habit of watching a piece of English news.
  我養成每天看一則英語新聞的習慣。

- We should make it a habit to plan for the next day before going to bed.
  = We should make a habit of planning for the next day before going to bed.
  我們應該養成習慣，在睡前先做好第二天的規劃。

- I make it a habit that the first thing I do on Saturday morning is jogging at the park.
  我養成一個習慣，每週六早晨起床第一件事情就是去公園慢跑。

2. 以it為虛受詞的句型之一，用來表示「促成……」的句型：

S＋make it possible (for＋sb.)＋to V

= S＋make＋N＋possible

- The Internet makes it possible for people in different countries to communicate through instant messaging.
  網路使位在不同國家的人們可以用即時通訊軟體溝通。

…d rail makes it possible for people to travel
…Kaohsiung in about 2 hours.

…人們可以在兩小時內從台北到高雄。

…advice made my plan more practicable.

他的建議讓我的計畫變得更加可能實現。

3. 以it為虛受詞的句型之一，用來表示「把某人或事物為理所
當然，忘了去珍惜或愛護」的句型：S＋take it for granted
that... 這個句型，是從take＋O＋for granted來的。如果只
要說一個簡單的事物，可以用名詞來表達的，就用take...for
granted。但是，如果需要講到一個子句才能表達的概念，則
用take it for granted that＋子句，也就是先用it做虛受詞，再
加上後面的that子句做真受詞。

4. take it for granted that＋S＋V 中的it為虛受詞，用來代替
that子句，it 可省略。受詞不是子句時，可用 take sb./ sth.
for granted 來表達；受詞過長時，亦可移到 granted 之後。

- Don't take it for granted that your friend will come to your
  rescue.
  不要以為你朋友來救你是理所當然。

- We could never take our parents' love and care for
  granted.
  我們不該把父母親的愛和關懷當成是理所當然的。

- Helen took it for granted that her team members would
  cover her job when she was absent.
  海倫以為團隊成員在她缺席時替她處理工作是理所當然的。

- Some patients took the devotion of the medical
  practitioners for granted.
  有些病患會認為醫療人員的投入是理所當然的。

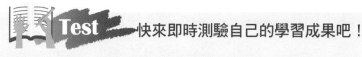

(   ) 1. Jerry took it for granted _____ .

(A) his parents help him with his homework

(B) that his friend would tolerate his rudeness.

(C) of receiving help from others

(D) his friend apologized to him

(   ) 2. I make it a rule _____ every day.

(A) going jogging   (B) of jogging

(C) to go jogging   (D) of jogging

(   ) 3. I found it soothing _____ every evening.

(A) with doing Yoga   (B) that he do Yoga

(C) by Yoga   (D) to do Yoga

(   ) 4. Researchers have proven it _____ to smoke.

(A) a threatening   (B) dangerous

(C) to hazard   (D) for damaging

(   ) 5. Carbon dioxide emission is _____ harmful to the environment.

(A) proven   (B) proven it

(C) that proven   (D) been proven

解答：(B) (C) (D) (B) (A)

ch
7
It
的
相
關
句
型

( ) 1. It is difficult to such a stubborn person like him _____.
    (A) that he accept advice   (B) accepting advice
    (C) of accepting advice   (D) to accept advice

( ) 2. It is urgent _____ the plastic waste in the ocean.
    (A) for eliminating   (B) that we should eliminate
    (C) the elimination of   (D) for we eliminating

( ) 3. It is kind _____ financial assistance to the poor family.
    (A) of you to offer   (B) for you offering
    (C) that you are offered   (D) to have offered

( ) 4. It is _____ my sister would come all the way from Canada to Taiwan to visit me.
    (A) what surprise (B) a surprise that   (C) kind of   (D) surprising to

( ) 5. It was a heart-broken story _____ during the class reunion.
    (A) that he told   (B) of him to tell
    (C) he had told   (D) that he will tell

( ) 6. It was David _____ guidance when I was lost.
    (A) which brought me   (B) who offered me
    (C) that he gave me   (D) for giving

( ) 7. It was unexpected _____ the project.
    (A) for leaving
    (B) the member's leaving
    (C) that a team member would leave
    (D) of the member to leave

( ) 8. Based on the outcome of inspection, the machine appeared _____ flaws in its electrical circuit.
    (A) to have had (B) that it has   (C) having   (D) to have

( ) 9. It makes little difference _____ we use a whiteboard or PowerPoint slides to make our presentation.

(A) until   (B) even tough   (C) whether   (D) if

( ) 10. It is queer that _____.

(A) he mistake the number   (B) the number mistaken

(C) the figure being miscalculated   (D) the figure should be miscalculated

( ) 11. It is imperative _____ a passport photo along with the resume to apply for the position.

(A) an applicant sending

(B) of an applicant to send

(C) that the applicant should send

(D) of an applicant sending

( ) 12. Rumor has it that _____.

(A) the politician is taking briberies from a foreign company

(B) the epidemic breaks out soon

(C) the limited-edition figurines sold out this morning

(D) the movie star cancel her trip to Asia

( ) 13. It _____ that I should send a gift to him as a token of gratitude.

(A) occurred to me   (B) struck on the thought

(C) hit upon an idea   (D) come up with the idea

( ) 14. It is of no use _____ flyers on the street. Few customers would be attracted by the ad.

(A) that you should issue   (B) issuing

(C) of us to issue   (D) to issue

( ) 15. Kevin found it was challenging _____ the employees from different departments for this project.

(A) that he should coordinate   (B) of him to coordinate

(C) coordinating   (D) to coordinate

ch

7

It 的相關句型

原來如此 系列 E260

這本句型最強效！英文滿分筆記
抓住重點快速攻克核心句型

常用句型解說╳練習題反覆演練

作　　者	李宇凡
顧　　問	曾文旭
社　　長	王毓芳
編輯統籌	耿文國、黃璽宇
主　　編	吳靜宜
執行主編	潘妍潔
執行編輯	吳芸蓁、吳欣蓉
美術編輯	王桂芳、張嘉容
法律顧問	北辰著作權事務所　蕭雄淋律師、幸秋妙律師

初　　版	2022年07月
出　　版	捷徑文化出版事業有限公司
電　　話	（02）2752-5618
傳　　真	（02）2752-5619

定　　價	新台幣320元／港幣 107 元
產品內容	1書

總 經 銷	采舍國際有限公司
地　　址	235 新北市中和區中山路二段366巷10號3樓
電　　話	（02）8245-8786
傳　　真	（02）8245-8718

港澳地區總經銷	和平圖書有限公司
地　　址	香港柴灣嘉業街12號百樂門大廈17樓
電　　話	（852）2804-6687
傳　　真	（852）2804-6409

▶本書部分圖片由 Shutterstock、freepik 圖庫提供。

捷徑Book站

現在就上臉書（FACEBOOK）「捷徑BOOK站」並按讚加入粉絲團，
就可享每月不定期新書資訊和粉絲專享小禮物喔！

http://www.facebook.com/royalroadbooks
讀者來函：royalroadbooks@gmail.com

國家圖書館出版品預行編目資料

這本句型最強效！英文滿分筆記，抓住重點快速
攻克核心句型 / 李宇凡著. -- 初版. -- 臺北市：捷
徑文化, 2022.07

　面；　公分. --（原來如此；E260）

ISBN 978-626-7116-14-2(平裝)

1. 英語　2. 句法

805.169　　　　　　　　　　　　　111009107